THE OCTOBER WITCH

When Julie Marsden's car breaks down in a Northumbrian mist, from Ninespears Crag, legendary resting-place of King Arthur and his Knights, a horseman with a falcon on his wrist rides to her rescue.

So starts this intriguing tale of mysterious happenings in and around the Crag. Has she fallen in love with a ghost dead for over eight hundred years? What is her role in the sinister human jigsaw where so many people are alarmed by her resemblance to Melanie, Adam Hebburn's missing wife?

THE OCTOBER WITCH

The October Witch

by
Alanna Knight

MAGNA PRINT BOOKS
Long Preston, North Yorkshire,
England.

British Library Cataloguing in Publication Data.

Knight, Alanna
   The October witch.
   I. Title
   823'.914(F)   PR6061.N45

   ISBN 0-86009-692-0

First Published in Great Britain by Hurst & Blackett Ltd, 1971

Copyright © 1971 by Alanna Knight

Published in Large Print 1985 by arrangement with the
Copyright holder.

Photoset in Great Britain by
Dermar Phototypesetting Co, Long Preston, North Yorkshire.

Printed and bound in Great Britain by
Redwood Burn Limited, Trowbridge, Wiltshire.

To my dear Mother
Gladys Lyall Cleet,
and
In loving memory of my Father
Herbert W. F. Cleet

CHAPTER 1

I was well and truly lost.

Not forty miles from home as might be travelled by an enterprising crow, with an expiring car on my hands and the end of a short cut which had added two frustrating hours to my journey from Edinburgh. Two hours of savage Northumbrian mist across treacherous Border moors, full of pot-holes, diminishing roads and unexpected streams.

The mini-car, used for genteel Sunday afternoon runs and family picnics, or at most a run down the Military Road into Newcastle to take Dad to the football match on a Saturday, was mortally offended by her present treatment. A creature of little courage, she coughed once and dramatically expired—by rolling into the ditch whose proximity I hadn't observed, and taking me with her. I scrambled out from the passenger's side, expecting a roaring wall of flame to follow the stench of petrol.

Imagination had been fed on too many

racing films. Nothing dramatic happened, except a small extra groan of protest from Mini, who lay with her off-side wheels gently whirring. She got no sympathy from me.

Swearing with unladylike ferocity, I took stock of a situation nothing short of appalling. I hadn't seen a single signpost since I left the main Edinburgh road. Doubtless they existed, littering every road-end—with their heads and shoulders conveniently shrouded in mist.

A few paces beyond the ditch was undoubtedly road. And very recently tarmacked. A heartening sight, for people in remote parts don't waste good rates on roads unlikely to justify their existence with good heavy traffic, constantly going somewhere.

I stamped my feet lovingly on its solid surface and set off hoping an A.A. box might spring from the murk, or some small monument indicating that civilisation had once lingered in this benighted land.

Looking skyward, I got an eyeful of mist and a coat-collar full of raindrops from the trees. Soon I would have another enemy.

Nightfall. A grim thought in this wilderness, although what passed for day, this blinding fog since Cheviot, meant only several shades of darker darkness. I swore again, taking heart from the sound of my voice. Geographically, I was on my home ground, my very own land of 'oak, and ash and bonny ivy-tree-ee'. Sentimental ballads were one thing heard in snug safe surroundings, but this North Country maid had small liking for the prospect before her.

I stopped, listened. Behind me the moors stretched endlessly, moors where wild birds cried and sheep lamented, and humans lost could perish with astonishingly little trace. Wishing I'd paid more attention to tracking at Girl Guide camps, I wondered what was the significance of trees with an alarming inward bent, stunted from birth by strong, bitter winds and high altitude. Mid-September and some were already stripped bare, their black branches croaking wheezily together, like witches with a bad case of laryngitis.

Perhaps there were houses near at hand. Not that I relished hammering on just any old door, with my tale of misfortune. However hospitable and normal the occupants, fog and mist bring strange fancies and I have a ripe imagination—'overripe' say my parents—nasty things click somewhat eagerly into it. Strange, horrid computations of gruesome things that go bump in the night ...

And suddenly, as if someone had flicked up

11

the corner of a curtain, the mist lifted for an instant. Long enough for Ninespears Crag to be clearly visible staring over my left shoulder.

Ninespears Crag. The flat-topped cone-shaped hill was unmistakable, visible from many angles, from many different Northumbrian roads, but I had never been this close before.

Ninespears Crag had an awe-inspiring reputation. The legendary burial place of King Arthur, who had more resting-places in Britain than Robert the Bruce's axe had new heads and handles.

It was all splendidly romantic to think about on a summer's day with cheerful birds singing, bees in clover, sunshine on stream. But on a witches' brew of a night like this the prospect of old Arthur and his Knights waiting around under that hill for the right moment to awaken, or, worse still, a ghostly evening canter down the road ...

Brrr. I shivered with more than cold and glanced apprehensively over my shoulder. I hoped their evening ride wouldn't be while I was walking here. I didn't give much for my chances as the earth shook under the hoofs of those great stamping horses.

My eyelashes were heavy with rain. I blinked

and Ninespears Crag had disappeared. I thought of all those Northumbrian legends—Grey Men, White Ladies, Brown Men. How I had loved them at school sitting by the cosy library fire, roasting forbidden chestnuts. Now they gave me the horrors.

Lately, the nightmare of sudden death had become an intimate part of my own life, gory inescapable death, with hospitals and grim-faced doctors and hours of grisly waiting for news. Since Charlie's death I had outgrown a taste for the macabre ...

The road moved downhill. Somewhere in front of me was the sea, the cold cruel North Sea. Perhaps the road ended on top of the cliff—a step out, and into nowhere. Feeling sorry for myself, I thought of the nice train, undeterred by fog, which had left Edinburgh, reached Berwick with its connecting bus to Corham hours ago. And I could have been on it. But no ...

'The car would be so useful,' I had said. For what? I wondered now, with parking as sorry a problem in Edinburgh as elsewhere?

I could have been sitting by the fire. Mum and Dad would be watching the news and the most serious of my concerns would be—was it my turn to wash the dishes? I kicked a stone savagely. It was all my own fault that I was on this damned blighted road. With the reckless self-confidence that makes L drivers newly graduated see themselves as rally driver-cum-Toad of Toad Hall, I had wheedled the car from Dad to visit the Edinburgh Festival and stay with Lucy, whose bridesmaid I had been in the spring. If Charlie hadn't died she would have been my matron of honour.

On the way home some madness tempted me to take the 'short cut', whip down to the coast and have a look at ancient Whitton Abbey. I had been taken there long ago, but the glossy pictures in books and on postcards in Dad's bookshop on the High Street in Corham were clearer to memory than childhood's visit when I was told: 'It rained and we never got our picnic.'

'Don't worry if I'm home late,' I told Mum on the phone from Edinburgh. 'I'll just meander—see the sights and take my time. Of course I'll drive carefully ...' See the sights, indeed. Some hope ...

Then I saw the tower.

In the poor visibility at first glance it was just another ruined peel tower, another dour survivor of the rollicking Border reivers and crafty Scots. I sighed. There would be no shelter in those uncompromising grey walls, the door somewhat inhospitably raised well above ground-level ...

But I was wrong. Drawing nearer, I saw this one was different. It wasn't even a ruin. Its ancient worn stones had been pointed, and recently too. Someone had hopefully planted trees, saplings protected by wire cages.

The garden gate was modern. But what raised my hopes to heaven, there were signs of habitation. Milk bottles on a wooden bench. Milk bottles in a bright yellow plastic container.

This must be Whitton Peel. And someone was undoubtedly at home. Almost certainly a telephone, and perhaps—a cup of coffee? Opening the gate, I rehearsed my speech to Dad. His precious new Mini. He had let me borrow her, because Charlie had died.

All my life, I thought, walking up the narrow path, my parents have been rushing to give me things. I should have been spoilt rotten, and probably was, until at some age a kind of social conscience raised itself from the mass of toys and pretty dresses, and said: 'Enough, Julie Marsden. You can't take for ever ...'

I remember subsequent forays—Oxfam, spastics, orphanages ... Why were my parents so indulgent? I wondered. Scared it was to make up for some deficiency in my character visible to their eyes only, some lack of understanding or deeply hidden insecurity, they feared I wasn't quite equipped to cope with.

Looking back over the years, instead of reasonable argument or an explanation to be avoided, it was always a present. A pram I could push, a puppy I could love. For intelligent people they behaved in the oddest way, motives unfathomable. They never learnt that love comes first, that they didn't have to keep on apologising for having an 'only child', that I would still have loved them had they been tinkers.

I rang the bell. The solid oak door on closer acquaintance had been somewhat freely modernised. Cheers—there was someone home.

Inside, a light glowed. I waited. Nothing happened.

With a faint shiver I rang again. A creepy place, right enough, with nothing but the sound of the trees, drip, drip, drip. It should have been homelier with those milk bottles. But didn't Dracula like milk too, when he couldn't lay hands on something more substantial? prompted glib imagination.

From this angle there was a discreet outcrop of telephone wires, a spiky television mast, incongruously nestling against a stern chimney built when Harry Hotspur was a lad. Glory be, the twentieth century had come to Whitton Peel with a vengeance.

At any other time I would have chuckled, but my throat was oddly dry. Despite renovations, I shivered, wishing I hadn't come, waiting, watching the silent tower with the mist and the overgrown garden crawling up to my heels.

A scraping sound inside. Oh, someone—at last. A footfall.

I rapped the door. 'Hello, hello?' Silence. 'Hello. Anyone at home?'

The scraping sounds ceased. Unnervingly, as if—as if someone listened on the other side of the door.

'Hello,' I said again, a shout this time. To comfort myself. I almost jumped out of my skin as the rookery above, becalmed by mist into an early bedding, rose into the air, filling the mist with darting black raggedy bodies and screams of rage, at this interruption of their domestic bliss.

I clutched the collar of my coat tight. My teeth were chattering. It was idiotic. Then suddenly I was angry. Angry that whoever was on the other side of the door hadn't the decency to open it to a benighted traveller. And a helpless girl at that ...

I raised my fist to the door. 'Can you help me? I'm lost,' I shouted, and felt like adding, 'I know you're there, watching me, because my scalp is prickling like mad.' Nothing but the silence came back.

(' "Is there anyone there?" said the Traveller, Knocking on the moonlit door ... "Tell them I came, and no one answered! ..." ')

It's a nasty habit remembering ghostly poems for all occasions. Only the moonlight was missing, the Listeners were very much in evidence ...

And suddenly what I had heard was without human origin. Even the most nervous old lady seeing the Traveller outside Whitton Peel, and hearing her cries of distress, would have been reassured by five foot four inches of Scared Stiff Young Female, weighing a hundred and ten pounds.

Nothing for it but to depart and look forward to a night in the ditch cosily tucked in with Mini. Wait. I listened again ...

This time there was no mistake. It *was* a dragging sound. ... Ghostly footsteps, perhaps clanking chains too ...

I fled down the garden path, retreat accompanied by the curses and complaints of rookery nook still circling wildly above my head.

Beyond the gate, heading for Mini, I turned and looked back. So much for the grand sightseeing tour of my native heath. On down that road, past Whitton Peel—I could smell the sea now. Heavy, seaweedy and rather dead—unpleasantly the air was full of the corpses of rotten fish. I shuddered.

That must be Whitton Sands. There was even a faint rhythmic beat of sea on shore. Hidden by mist, the Priory must lie just beyond that belt of trees crouching on the cliff-top. Well, it could keep its connections with Scott's *Marmion* and I no longer yearned to see the famous Crusader's Tomb. With the Phantom of the Tower breathing down my neck, my taste for the surge of history had run cold. I wanted pop music, neon lights, central heating, a hot bath.

I started back up the road. On my right now, Ninespears Crag completely devoid of mist seemed uncomfortably near, larger and more oppressive than before, as if it had taken advantage of my visit to Whitton Peel to tiptoe softly across the moor. One of the mist's little tricks, I knew, but not particularly inviting, this suggestion of mountains moving unaided ...

'The night has a thousand eyes,' whispered

imagination, with ghastly promptness. It had indeed, and all of them were crawling up my back at that moment. From Whitton Peel, with its uncharitable occupant, to King Arthur in his last resting-place.

'They sleep,' says legend, 'eight knights and Arthur, spears at the ready, awaiting the call to ride out to defend their native land ...' Well, poor old Britain, surtaxed, devalued, decimal-coined, she would never need him more than now.

Then I heard it.

Out of the mist. Horses' hoofs, heavy, busy, angry. The clink of harness, sword. The creak of saddle. The ground beneath my feet shook.

Horsemen.

And riding down the road, riding straight for me ...

King Arthur ...

He leaned forward in his saddle, gold on his hair. The horse reared, plunged, screamed. Frightened, real as myself. Then, immense, larger than life, the horseman. A white shirt, dark trousers and riding boots—the shirt open down to the waist even in weather like this, I thought, ridiculously prosaic ... He leaped down at me, blinking wet mist off thick eyelashes and I saw that it wasn't a gold crown on his head at all, just an illusion of mist on russet-coloured hair, more red than brown and curling.

The curly hair was the only kind thing about a narrow craggy face, high forehead, hooked nose and wide cheekbones which cut across the planes of his face, giving it dignity, power and ruthlessness. His eyes under jutting brows were narrow, blue and so wide-spaced they looked inhuman. Inhuman as those of the falcon, screaming blue murder, its great dark wings flapping round and round the man's gloved fist.

Even as I turned to fly he caught me effortlessly, I was face to face with him, half-strangled by one strong arm.

'Damn you,' he said through narrowed lips. 'Damn you—I thought I was rid of you for ever ... What sepulchre in hell opened and let you loose again?'

Huge, he towered over me. He could have snapped my spine, throttled me with one hand. More than six foot tall, built to match. A Borderer, straight from the ranks of Harry Hotspur, from the savage high-cheekboned face to the strong, powerful body. That imprisoning arm, vice-like, real enough to dismiss any thoughts of a spectral King Arthur and reduce me to gibbering terror.

'Let go!' I screamed. 'Let me go.'

And suddenly he smiled. A radiant smile, so totally unexpected in that rock of a face, so utterly delightful that I almost forgot indignation.

'I'm sorry,' he said, releasing me, 'I thought you were someone else ...'

'A friend, no doubt,' I said nastily.

He chuckled, looked me over, head on one side. But the smile, the laugh, didn't ring true any more. The horseman was worried, bewildered. If it hadn't seemed silly, I would have said he was scared to death.

The falcon was nervous too and near enough to anchor me with one chummy claw on my arm. 'Would you mind ...' I said to it coldly. But it stared back, eyes wide and unblinking, looking into my face, somehow unnervingly like its master.

'Would you mind,' I said to the horseman, 'asking your—beast—to remove its restraining mit? Or am I marked down for tomorrow's dinner?'

'Hereward,' he said sternly. 'Desist.' And to me, in surprised tones: 'He likes you.' To which Hereward gave the birdlike equivalent of a heavy sigh, retreated to crouch again on the gloved fist and fluttered his plumage like a disappointed dowager.

With some difficulty I tried to remember that this was a perfectly ordinary evening. In Northumberland, not wildly addicted to romance, and not forty miles from home. The time: the twentieth century.

God help me—ancient sweet dear God who made us all—help me, deliver me from falconers, hunting parties, and King Arthur's ghost—out on a night like this ...

'Was that your car curled up in the ditch back there?' he asked.

'Yes. I'm lost. How do I get back to the Corham road?'

He nodded in the direction of the horse. 'Up you come and I'll take you up to the car.'

I paled at the thought of clambering up on to that enormous horse's back, the indignity of a tight skirt. Neither need have worried me.

All in one swift movement he had me up beside him, without even disturbing a feather of Hereward, who eyed me with placid satisfaction. And, I could have sworn, a knowing wink. Oh Lord ...

'He looks as if you do this every evening,' I said. 'Now I understand about those Border raiders.'

His smile was vague, his mind elsewhere, and taking out a darling tiny leather hood, with a

23

gay bold feather in it, he bonneted Hereward. 'That'll keep him quiet.'

As we cantered along the road, I said: 'Terribly sorry to put you about.' I'd better be nice to him, use some feminine wiles. I wanted to get Mini back on the road and only a big strong man could do that. He didn't answer, so I asked: 'Where are the rest of the party?'

'Which party?'

I indicated the hooded Hereward: 'The hunt.'

Now he smiled, easily, playing me along: 'Away to the Chase, of course.'

'Chevvy Chase?'

He chuckled. 'Local lass, eh? Know your history?'

'Indeed I do. What's more, I think I've had an encounter just before you came along, with Merlin.'

He looked down into my face and whistled softly. 'No kidding,' he said laughing. 'Do tell me.'

'When Mini went into the ditch I walked down the road to find help. I found this weirdie tower and evidence of a telephone. There were signs of life in plenty—sounds inside—milk bottles on the step and so forth. I rang and hammered on the door, but nobody came. And I knew fine well they were watching me,' I added proudly. 'Anyway, the whole thing gave me the creeps. There was something about that place—oh, I dare say it's all very ordinary in sunshine but on a misty evening ...' I shivered. 'You don't have a tame ghost hereabouts, by any chance?'

'Not that I know of.' He frowned. 'Tower, you said?' And gave it a moment's thought. 'On the left? That would be Whitton Peel. An old man, a hermit, lives there. That's your answer —he would certainly never open his door to a girl, especially a young and pretty one like yourself.'

His tone was light, outrageously flirtatious. I should have been consoled except that there was something forced, nervous and uncertain, about the whole episode. As if he were trying desperately hard to create a good impression. Shortly he would be pretending that the Strangulation Scene had been mere heavy-handed teasing ...

Very conscious of this warm underclad man beside me, I thoughtfully stroked Hereward's back feathers. Hereward turned his head, beak half-open, as if he'd like to contribute something to the conversation, if only he knew the words.

Then there was Mini. On her back with two

wheels still pawing the air. Ah, she wouldn't be much trouble to this man, I thought, as he lifted me down from the horse. Then I sniffed the air. 'Petrol,' I said. 'Do be careful.'

He smiled, over his shoulder. 'It's all right, nothing to panic about. Just some slopped out of the tank.' As he grappled with the car, I watched in silent horror, expecting flames to shoot forth any moment. With my terror of fire, nothing in this world would have induced me to get inside, start that engine.

Mini was safely on the road, on all her four wheels. 'It's all yours,' said my rescuer, dusting his hands. 'What's wrong?'

'Petrol. That smell. I'm sorry—I just daren't start the engine. I have this thing about fire,' I ended lamely.

A 'thing' was putting it mildly. It was a fetish, a primeval terror. And ironically precognitive, considering that Charlie had died from burns when his motor-bike hit a tree and exploded in a wall of fire, as he drove away from me, in a temper, after our quarrel. Always the final secret words that nobody—his family or mine—would ever know. Only I would be haunted, taunted for all eternity.

The horseman clicked finger and thumb, a gesture demanding keys. Somehow he managed to get his long body behind the steering wheel. The engine promptly sprang to life. But no fire ...

Two minutes later we had said cheery good-byes. I had thanked him profusely and he had painstakingly shown me on the map how I couldn't miss the road to Corham. As I moved off, he held up a hand in farewell and when I looked in the car mirror the road was empty.

All three of them, man, horse and falcon, swallowed by mist. As if they had never been ... And I had reached the signpost he told me about, and had Mini's nose turned towards home, before I remembered I didn't know his name.

The mist ended precisely two miles due south of Ninespears Crag. The road was deserted. I hadn't seen one living soul when I touched a tiny village, one street with a dozen houses and a small general shop. It was open, and it sold everything, including cigarettes.

I waited patiently at the counter as the echoing sound of noisy doorbell faded. Face to face with myself in a mirror, strategically placed so that customers—and their intentions—were clearly visible from the little parlour.

At least I was still the same, I thought with relief, a rather battered and untidy version of the girl who had left Lucy's pretty new house in Corstorphine this morning. I tidied the white headscarf and tucked wisps of lank dark hair out of sight. Squatting, I turned my eyes into black smudges. On passports, etc., I hopefully wrote against 'Eye colour': 'Blue'.

('They're not blue,' hissed Lucy, 'they're purple, like pansies')

I kept on determinedly writing 'Eyes—blue'. It was absurd, I'd never met anyone in my life with purple eyes. Violet, sapphire, never purple. I felt rather ashamed. And apologetic that the great spikes of black eyelashes were really me, when they looked so undeniably fake.

'Hello, pet,' said the very old lady who tottered to the counter, her knitting needles in one hand. 'How are ye the day? Cigarettes ...' She plonked down twenty of a rather more expensive brand than I usually buy. 'Here ye are, lass. Your usual ones.'

A trade gimmick, I thought, crafty old dear. And said firmly: 'I'm economising. I'll take those other ones.'

She grinned. 'Money a bit tight again, pet? Ay, cost of living goes up every day.' And as she counted out change she looked at me curiously. 'Been keeping all right, pet? Haven't seen you for a while now.'

28

I went out feeling shaken. The old girl must be in her dotage. Or else that chummy familiarity was a sound trick some of those superior shops in Corham village would have done well to adopt.

By the time Corham crossroads came into view, I was practically convinced that I had encountered a knight from the past. Even his accent didn't belong in twentieth-century Northumberland. A knight out of Ninespears Crag for an airing, to rescue a lady in true Arthurian tradition, complete with falcon. I felt rather proud. It was one of those weird experiences of extra-sensory perception so popular these days. An encounter with times past as I had always wished it would happen to me ... How super to travel back in time, to see the world as it was, fresh and young.

'But there isn't a scratch on Mini anywhere,' said Warren Browne, half an hour later, kicking at her wheels. Warren is Charlie's elder brother, who abandoned the family farming tradition to be a policeman. He always acts as if everything and everybody should be treated with suspicion. That has nothing to do with being a policeman, it's just in his nature. He did it even when we were kids. Preferring gay light-hearted Charlie, it was flattering to know

29

both brothers were in love with me. But I should have had sense somewhere along the way to recognise that preference isn't love ...

Now despairingly I realised, as Warren hovered eternally about our house and garden, that he was waiting for a decent interval before he, in his turn, proposed. Both families would be so pleased. Sentimental Mrs. Browne and, in particular, my armchair detective father, always agog for Warren's stories about crimes—sitting there with his scrapbook on criminology, gathered over the years: *An Anthology of Border Badmen*. The book he would write—someday. Yes, indeed, Warren would have his uses to my family. And I liked and respected him. No doubt I would make a competent country policeman's wife. Only I saw myself with youth fled, in the fading years of middle age, looking out across these hills of home and realising what I had missed in life. That I had never known the meaning of a love I would die for ...

'Falcon, did you say?' asked Warren doubtfully. 'Oh, aye, and what did this horseman look like?'

'Big, reddish curly hair, aquiline face. A medieval face. Somebody out of Chevy Chase., Or the Earl of Bothwell?'

'Who?' Warren frowned, ready to take out his

30

notebook for a detailed description.

'Oh, never mind,' I said shortly. 'Now promise you won't tell the parents. They'll make one almighty fuss. Bad enough crashing Mini ...'

At home Dad would ask: 'What was this man like?' As if the Horseman were Frankenstein on the look-out for victims. 'What did you go and knock on that door for—*anybody* might live there.' And Mum would say: 'Getting up on a horse—in that skirt. I don't know how you dared. And a strange man. He might have taken you *anywhere.*'

The implication being that I had gone out asking to be murdered and narrowly escaped rape. If I'd told them about the Strangulation Scene, Dad would have been in a high old frenzy: Heavens, I saw him dialling the police: 'My daughter was assaulted ...'

'There, there, I won't say a word,' said Warren soothingly, and patted my shoulder. Tall and thin and dark. Not handsome, but lively-looking and all the girls in Corham thought he was 'super'. The fellows liked him too. A great line in funny stories which he told well, he liked a game of football at the Jubilee Park on a Saturday afternoon and a pint in the pub at night. There was nothing upstage about

31

Warren. And though Corham grieved for Charlie, who was handsome and wild and clever and went to the University, they secretly thought that Warren was the better man (according to my friend Lucy, anyway).

'Here, I'm on duty and you'll get a parking ticket if you don't move on, Julie Marsden.' Warren looked at me and then at the sky. 'Funny thing, weather's been fine here all day, no mist mentioned on the weather report either.' He chuckled. 'God, Julie, you should have been an actress—you always had such an imagination. Sure you didn't take the wrong turning and meet a miner on a bike, carrying a canary?'

'Oh shut up,' I said ungraciously. I was furious because I had a funny feeling, too, that the Horseman didn't exist. Bring him to Corham High Street and he'd vanish. As I drove off I said: 'I wasn't seeing things—what's more, I intend going back to Whitton Sands on a decent day and exploring that Peel Tower. You can come with me, if you like.'

'Not likely,' grinned Warren.

'Stay at home, then.' As I waited for the traffic lights to change, I thought, if my Horseman were just a ghost, then this brave new world was a sadder place for women, deprived of the sheer animal magnetism that he exuded. Maybe those romances in the Middle Ages, which always sounded a bit stuffy, had something after all, with men the image of my Horseman roaming loose about the countryside.

The parents were at the Community Centre playing bridge. I didn't wait up for them. Reaction had made me strangely tired. Healthily tired. I didn't need those sleeping pills—and the instant sleep, quite dreamless, they offered—to take away my hag-ridden guilty nightmares about Charlie's death.

Perhaps the night of mist at Ninespears Crag was the turn of the tide. So much happened, with such swiftness afterwards.

I discovered that you can live with situations for years, accepting them and never once suspecting the truth that is right there staring you in the face. Afterwards it seemed sometimes that the encounter on the road to Whitton Sands had unleashed an evil genie into my life, waiting, bottled up, for the moment to strike ...

How often I had told myself since Charlie died that his death was the worst that could happen to me. Even if I never found another love I could be content. For I had Mum and Dad and the security of a happy home where I was the loved and rather spoiled only child.

Lightning doesn't strike twice, they say ...

But two days after my meeting with the Horseman half of my world fell away.

I learned that the Marsdens weren't my parents at all ...

CHAPTER 2

The evening began in the best traditions of modern domestic drama.

The newspapers had been read, Mum's knitting pattern and what we were going to eat tomorrow had been thoroughly discussed. Our favourite television serial was just over and, without waiting for the news, Dad switched off and said:

'Julie. Mum has something to tell you. Never mind about coffee yet ... Sit down, there's a good lass.'

He looked so solemn, I sat down, hearing my own heartbeat. It was something about Charlie. Something horrible. A death-note blaming me had been found. That was one steady nightmare, the other finding I had to go on with the wedding—to a dead man.

'About—about Charlie?' I whispered.

Mum came across the settee and took my hands. 'No, darling. It's about us.'

Dad was bankrupt, I thought wildly. They

were getting a divorce. Then I listened. Realised with delight that it had nothing to do with fears for parents or terror about Charlie.

'You see, dear,' Mum said, playing with the wrist-watch they had given me for Christmas, and thus avoiding my eyes, 'you see, Dad and I could never have any children. And there weren't any miracles in my day. No fertility drugs. We'd been married six years, I'd had several operations ...'

Suddenly, in a swift rush of words, her hands stopped moving. I stared at her, wondering if she was teasing me. Saying I was adopted. That I was illegitimate.

Illegitimacy is no shock in these days. The product of a permissive society, I did faithful lip-service to a whole lot of way-out theories affirmed by my friends. Protected by the herd, I would never have dared put any of those theories to the test. For instance, no with-it girl of twenty-four, like me, could ever have held up her head again if she admitted to still being a virgin after a three-year-long engagement.

Yes, illegitimacy should have been less than a shock—and here was the reason for all those presents, too lavish, too often, throughout the years. Now I knew why they were so anxious, the dear darling parents, to make amends. Bless their hearts, they needn't have worried ...

At my side, Mum sniffed, wiped away a tear. At the fireplace, Dad watched my face intently, lit a pipe. Turning, I hugged Mum, rushed over and threw myself into Dad's arms.

'You don't mind?' said Mum breathlessly. 'You aren't *upset* at all?'

'Of course I'm not. Do you really think knowing you hadn't personally brought me into this world could stop me loving you? That it could make the slightest difference to you both being the *greatest* parents? Silly, silly darlings—why didn't you tell me years ago?'

They exchanged a glance. Dad cleared his throat, said warily: 'We intended telling you when you got married.'

'But then—when Charlie ...' Mum choked on the words. 'Oh, Julie, it's all been so awful for you. We just couldn't ...'

'I know, darling, I know,' I said, sparing her. Thinking how terrible it had been—for Charlie. I stood up. 'Well, now the great confession is over—how about coffee?'

In the kitchen, setting the supper tray, piling chocolate biscuits on a plate, I stopped suddenly. I was singing under my breath. Singing. I must be in a state of delayed shock. Nothing else short of complete heartlessness could explain my feeling of normality.

The feeling that I had always—somehow—known.

They were absolutely delighted, idiotically grateful for my attitude. Later I heard them talking in the bedroom. Dad saying: 'She was always such a sensible lass. And to think we'veworried ourselves all these years ...'

I went in to say good night, for the bedtime kiss I remembered all my life. 'I'm very glad you chose me. Very flattered and very grateful. Adopted or real, you're the dearest, nicest parents in the whole world.'

As I got ready for bed, taking off my make-up at the old familiar mirror, I picked up a photo of Mum. It was my favourite, a coloured one taken with Charlie's first enthusiasm for a new and expensive camera. Strange, I thought, looking at my own reflection, how alike we were. Only our eyes were a different colour—the dark hair, the set of features identical.

In her early fifties, Mum still looked young. Young enough to be delighted when new friends said: 'Gosh, she looks like your older sister.'

Wondering, I remembered now a score of

memories. 'This must be your little girl, Mrs Marsden, she's so like you ...'

Charlie's mother chuckling saying I was Mum's 'spitting image'. I wondered if the Brownes knew ...

Well, I thought, climbing into bed, I suppose people who live together and love each other take on a sort of likeness. It was probably gestures, voice, more than real resemblance. It was strange to lie awake listening to the lonely sounds of night—a train's whistle, a bird's wild echoing call, a wind outside stirring the roses.

Strange to wonder where my real parents were. Were they alive or dead? What tragic drama had made marriage impossible? When I had asked Mum and Dad about them they said, avoiding each other's eyes: 'We got you from an adoption society. One of their rules, they don't reveal the true parents' identity ...'

Consoling, if I needed consolation. But I had a curious feeling they knew more than they were telling. All this excitement was too much for me and as I lay waiting for the sleeping pill to take effect, I wondered what brief sad love, wild and passionate, in some forgotten summer hedgerow, had brought me unwanted—dreaded —into this world. I saw a young girl, at her wits' end, praying to God she was wrong.

That she had just miscalculated, there was a reason for delay—flu, a stomach upset. And then, with that first bout of uncontrollable morning sickness, knowing for certain she was pregnant. Wondering how long she could conceal it, get rid of it, tell her parents ...

I thought of her shadowy lover. Someone magnetic. He turned into a man on a white horse, and in my dreams I felt the strong arms ... There were lips too, and thighs, and a warm strong body. And so I slept, thinking of a man I would never meet again. The Horseman from Ninespears Crag.

I began to see him everywhere.

Imagination plays strange tricks and so do erotic dreams. Once when I had been home almost a week, I was setting some books in the shop window. I looked up, saw a russet-coloured leonine head driving a sleek white Kharmann Ghia through the winding High Street. It was a sunny day, the hood was down and it moved slowly. Like someone searching for a street number. Or a shop.

Trying for a better look, I clumsily sent the display of the latest best-seller spinning. Rushed to the door. Too late. Heart thumping, I set the books to rights again, feeling foolish, my hands trembling.

The broad back, the wide shoulders, seemed unmistakable. But the driver could hardly be a stranger. The retreating car had Northumbrian registration plates. It was a trick of my imagination. Besides, Corham was well out of the way for a traveller from Whitton Sands. Berwick, Newcastle or even Edinburgh would be the place to shop, to eat. Certainly not Corham, with its two main streets, the old Square, the Abbey, the Roman camp by the river.

After that first day I kept careful watch, without any plan of what I would do, or say, if I met my Horseman face to face. Once I rushed out of the shop when the now familiar white car stopped a few yards away at the traffic lights.

I stood on the pavement edge, looking hard at the driver, but today with the sun in his eyes he wore dark glasses, most of his face hidden by a turned-up collar. My heart, thumping like a drum, said: 'It's him.' I stood there out of my head with delight, grinning like a fool, willing him to recognise me. As the car moved off, he turned his head slightly; but not a muscle of his face moved ...

I ran back into the shop, my face scarlet. I must be going mad. No sane girl falls in love—if this *was* love, this tumult of emotion, of wild dreams—with a man who half-strangled her on their first meeting.

Kinky, I thought—and how ...

Working every day with Dad in the book-shop, he noticed my chronic absent-minded-ness, but bless his heart, doubtless put it down to 'her bit of a shock'.

After that display of idiocy on the pavement, I grew wary. But not wary enough. Every pass-ing white car caught the corner of my eye, I was constantly looking towards the window. When next I saw the car I had accosted at the traffic lights, with my grins and nods, again the hood was down. But russet-head wasn't alone. This time he had a female, with long fairish hair, both of them ageless behind dark glasses. Wife, daughter, girl-friend?

Angrily I stamped back to a waiting cus-tomer, pretending a search for a somewhat obscure book in the stacks. You deserve every-thing you get, I told myself, fancying a man like that.

Knowing my reason depended on telling someone, I telephoned Lucy in Edinburgh that evening, while the parents were out.

'You were probably right first guess,' she said. 'Probably a farmer, married with half a dozen kids.' She chuckled. 'I expect he had a tumble in the hay with a milkmaid, then sent her packing. When he saw you in the murk at Ninespears Crag—all girls in white headscarves probably look alike to him—so he made a mistake, thought she was back to plague him ...'

'But it was him, Lucy. In the car outside the bookshop. I'm sure, even with dark glasses, I couldn't be mistaken.'

'Of course it was, ducky. But you could hardly expect him to acknowledge you. Be reasonable, the poor man was probably dying of embarrassment.'

'Well, why does he keep on coming to Corham, then?'

'Julie dear,' she said patiently, 'he has probably been driving through Corham, up and down the High Street, for years and years. But *you* never noticed him until now—until that meeting at Ninespears Crag brought him into your range of vision, so to speak.' She paused. 'He certainly made an impression on you. Good gracious.'

'That meeting made an impression on him too, Lucy. His exact words were: 'What sepulchre in hell opened and let you loose again? I thought I was rid of you for ever!'

At the other end of the line, Lucy gasped. 'How very nasty. He must be an absolute horror—I hope you didn't tell your dad. He would have thrown a fit ...'

When I rang off I was not much consoled. Was I right or was Lucy? Did my Horseman come to Corham deliberately? What was he looking for? 'A sepulchre in hell' and a girl he thought he was 'rid of for ever'? Or did I haunt him—my ghost—as he haunted me?

Lucy had said: 'You're being ridiculous. I'd forget the whole thing if I were you. A farmer with six kids, remember.'

But the part did not compute. Gentle Northumberland farmers, devoted to a family, didn't go round wanting to strangle strange girls. Whatever the identity of my Horseman, of one thing I was certain. He wasn't in this for laughs. He was involved in some drama of appalling magnitude ...

Perhaps it was the very mystery of it all that attracted me, a very ordinary girl moth with her very dull commonplace life, rushing towards a bright flame. And knowing perfectly well what lies in wait for headstrong, heedless moths ...

They never even smell the flame that burns them. Dead ...

I remember the following days with the intense

clarity that in retrospect marks happiness never to be recaptured. There was absolutely no premonition that this phase of my life was soon to end.

Although the calendar said autumn, that September continued a pretence of summer in long sunny, tranquil days. In the garden of No. 6 The Cloisters, a romantic name for our six-year-old villa in a rather dull suburban avenue, roses bloomed, and in the evenings when shadows lengthened, turning Dad's neat lawns to emerald velvet, their perfume filled the air.

One day Dad lifted the secateurs and listened. The sky was strangely silent, with no more twisting, darting flights against its endless blue.

'Aye, the swallows have gone,' he said. 'Summer's over.'

It seemed incredible to me that their built-in radar saw beyond the rich windless days, the still drowsy fields and mellow bronzed stillness, to the longer shadows that heralded the death-bed of summer.

'Listen to the blackbirds, they know fine well what's happening,' said Dad. Already the twilit garden was full of fierce, black, secret movements as they shrilly disputed with warning 'chk, chk' their territorial rights. 'As it was,' said Dad, lighting a pipe and watching the smoke spiral fade, 'as it has been for thousands of years. And,' watching the great white ribbon of a jet racing across the sky, 'with God's help, as it shall be for whatever time man has left to him.'

Mum came out smiling, wiping floured hands on her pinny. 'Do you two want cheese scones for supper?'

And the smell of that baking lingers for me, among the roses, to this day. I can feel still the warmth of Dad's arm tucked into mine as we went into the kitchen, and the smell of Mum's face powder. It was some old-fashioned brand she clung to when most of us scorned loose powder and its perfume was one of my earliest recollections.

After supper Dad said: 'Aye, now that the garden will be needing less attention, we'll have to get back to The Book again, Julie.'

Mum and I exchanged secret smiles. He said that every autumn. Writing The Book was always to be his winter-into-spring activity. But *Border Badmen*, with its assortment of criminals north and south of the Cheviots, remained a scrapbook of clippings.

Yet for the first time I believed him. There was such harmony inside the house, never the shade of bickering or discontent, so that any dream seemed possible. Everything went perfectly. No toast burned, no dishes were broken. I put it all down to the fact that September was a sentimental time for the parents, who had married in the Abbey Church thirty years ago, and were still lovebirds.

I surprised myself by taking kindly to Warren's evening visits and felt flattered at having so faithful a friend. As we walked down to the river past haystacks which, like so many giant blond wigs threw long dramatic shadows over the stubble fields, our conversation was the inevitable: 'Do you remember ...'

Any other life than Corham for the rest of my days seemed unimaginable, a life away from the people dear to me too abhorrent to contemplate, and when Warren took my arm, or held my hand, I smiled, lingered instead of hurrying away with a swift change of subject on to less personal topics.

Even the bookshop had its corner of my heart. Soon the autumn books would be arriving. Straight from the publishers in great fat exciting parcels. I'd been in love with books all my life. The new crisp ones, shiny-jacketed, spines straight, crackling as they opened, spilling out new ideas, new worlds, endearing as chickens from eggs. Sitting in a corner of the bookshop was one of my earliest recollections. Lack of pictures never bothered me even then, my love was already a sensual thing—of smell and touch. Then I learned to love the old musty second-hand shelves, to take down books spotted with damp, their pages marked by insect corpses, or a withered rose leaf, some long-dead lover's token. I opened the pages to the summer sun of two hundred years ago, to elusive fragrances of snuff, patchouli ...

But summer dies. Toast burns, dishes crack. And lives break. As mine would do, when I felt most secure in this continuity of time, love and affection. Since my encounter with the Horseman, I was secretly a little hopeful that my heart wasn't too broken to mend and that a tormented conscience might yet lie at peace. Looking at Warren, thinking how nice he was, I thought—and hoped—that some day I might indeed fall in love with him.

Then abruptly, with us all in our places, our words learned, the stage and lighting set for a quiet autumn, Fate moved in ...

It began a day in no way different from a thousand others. Lady Ester Pleys telephoned, saying she had made a choice from the monthly book list we circulated to regular customers and would I take round a selection that evening?

I was always glad of an excuse to visit Pleys Castle. Glad of Mini, too, I thought, on such occasions, turning her nose down the one-mile-long rhododendron drive that lay two miles down-river from Corham. There was nothing of Border keep about this gracious Georgian manor-house, with neat green lawns pressing down to a tree-lined river walk. Its grounds were now maintained by the National Trust, and the house too was open to the public on certain afternoons in summer.

I don't remember early National Trust visits, although my parents told me I had been taken there before the age of ten, when I won the school prize for recitation. Perhaps that accounted for the odd familiarity. Lady Ester, one of the school governors, pressed a book token into my hand and those of the three runner-ups. But I wasn't impressed by her speech about how good, how talented, we all were, I was much more interested in the entrance, the great hall. I had the oddest feeling that I knew them well. I didn't like it, there was something sinister, as if I struggled with a time long-past and an elusive memory.

I went out, the girls following, twittering. Someone said: 'Gosh, wait till I tell my mam, Lady Ester's not a witch, after all.'

' 'Course she's not, you daft nit, she's a recluse,' I said, and the girls stared at me in awe. Nobody knew what a recluse was and neither did I then. They shouted: 'Oh, c'm on,' but still I lingered, wondering when I had run a small questing finger along the rose carvings of the ancient fireplace, and why the great hall had shrunk in size.

In recent years the hall has been dominated by a life-size portrait of Hector Pleys, Lady Ester's nephew. Since the revival of old movies on television, both the portrait and Hector's grave in the Castle grounds have become tourist meccas. The painting shows him in his greatest part, as King Arthur. It was painted by a local artist, Adam Hebburn, and has those marvellous eyes that follow the viewer wherever he goes.

'Talk of the devil and Pleys Castle,' said Dad, the week after my last visit to Lady Ester. 'I wonder if she knows they're bringing back one of Hector's early films, *Bitter Harvest.*' He handed Mum the *Radio Times.* 'Remember it, May?'

'I do indeed. I wept buckets. You must see it, Julie. Hector Pleys was the star of our young day. Marvellous voice, quite incredibly handsome.'

But this time Mum didn't cry, either because television movies never seem quite as real as they do in the cinema or because the style of acting had subtly changed and a cruel twist in the years can turn great drama into melodrama. Oh, the good looks, the liquid eyes and velvet voice were there, but I thought the whole thing a bit of a yawn. Hector Pleys was too pretty for my taste, the 'thirties' convention a giggle that demanded even rough sailors or starving miners be played by public schoolboys labouring under the dreadful handicap of Harrow accents.

'It was one of his very early films,' said Mum with a sigh, apologising for Hector as Dad switched over for the news. 'He really was a great actor when he matured a bit. Not so bonny.'

'Right enough,' said Dad. 'When they got a bit of meat on his bones and his face looked as if it had been lived in. Remember when we went all the way to Newcastle that snowy night to see him as King Lear on the stage, May? And you didn't like it, because he wasn't young and handsome and it had a sad ending?' Dad chuckled.

Next week the Sunday newspaper advised television addicts to see him in his greatest role, as King Arthur in *Sunrise at Avalon.*

'They must have bought up a batch of his films,' said Mum. 'And you *must* see this one, Julie.'

'Oh, Mum, Warren and I are going to Berwick,' I grumbled.

But we came back early and I remember nothing but the awe of watching that superb dateless performance. I grieved for Hector Pleys and that the world should lose such an actor. Even through the grainy-grey picture I understood his greatness, the maturity and bewildering power of voice range—using pitch and tone like an opera singer to hold an audience spellbound. If Hector Pleys had recited the alphabet his audience would still have shouted 'Encore'. I'm not a sentimental filmgoer, I rarely shed a tear—but that night I cried. And I was furious with Dad for putting coal on the fire and Warren for offering me a cigarette.

As for sex-appeal, Hector Pleys had it all. Good for old Mum, I thought, she knew an exciting man when she saw one. We're apt to forget that sex fascinated our parents too. No wonder the women went mad—at that quizzical smile, the raised eyebrows—the shivers started down my spine.

What an athlete, too. Leaping here, there, everywhere. And sometimes when he jumped on to a horse I found my heart banging away like a sledgehammer. Back view he was like my Horseman, who undoubtedly, ghost or real, also had sex-appeal. There was even a falcon, the image of Hereward, staring straight out of the screen.

'How did he die?' I asked Mum, as we made coffee, both still rather dazed. I knew something vague about accident or illness ...

'His ending was pure theatre,' said Mum with a sigh. 'More dramatic, some said, than even his colourful life warranted. It must be at least fifteen years ago—he was making a film on location in Africa. Got snake-bite and had a million-to-one allergy to the serum. He was dead within hours. All very horrible, paralysed, swollen up beyond recognition, I read somewhere. Anyway, they flew him home to be buried at Pleys and practically all the great stars, stage and screen, attended the memorial service in the Abbey.'

'Was there a wife, family?'

'Nobody. Only Lady Ester. The title goes to a remote cousin after she dies, Hector wasn't directly in line. He was married twice, twice divorced. Plenty of paternity suits, too, and scandals, I seem to remember. But, despite it all, no heirs—well, not legitimate ones, anyway.'

At Pleys Castle, Lady Ester was more erratic than usual. She twittered about books I'd brought, changed her mind a dozen times, fingered them all suspiciously, asked: 'Have you read them, Julie? Are they really worth the money? Books are getting so expensive—everything costs a fortune these days ...'

She lost her glasses which I found down the side of her chair. She lost the notes she had written the titles on. She seemed so wild-eyed and distrait I decided the old girl was going gaga at last, poor dear, she would never keep this mausoleum going much longer, National Trust or no.

'Have you a moment?' she asked, as I got up to leave, taking all but three of the books I had brought back with me. 'Perhaps you would like tea, but the maid is out.'

'Let me make you some,' I offered cheerfully, wondering how on earth I'd find the way to the kitchen.

She fluttered a hand. 'No, no—not at all. Do sit down, please. I wonder,' and her eyes darted round my head as if I were being attacked by an unseen swarm of wasps, 'I wonder,' she said, leaning forward and dropping her voice to a tiny hoarse whisper, 'if you could be spared ...'

For one horrible moment I thought I was

being asked to move in and attend to the deficiencies of the maid's absence. As general factotum.

'You see, Julie, I have this friend. A very dear lady. And she's a writer. Does superb nature books. She's working on wild flowers at this moment. Quite desperately needs someone to do an index, a bibliography. Your father has told me often how good you are at gathering data, at cataloguing. As you know, I'm most interested in his little crime book, most interested ...' She paused, fingering the booklist, her choice all thrillers of the old-fashioned type. 'I wonder, with all your experience, if you could be spared to help her out. You see, the poor darling is something of an invalid. Doesn't get around at all well. Only for two weeks, you understand.' She waited, watching me eagerly.

'And the salary would be, er, well worth your while.'

I didn't feel coarse enough to enquire 'How much?' and thought gloomily about the local writers who patronised our bookshop. An overworked, underpaid, penniless lot, always hotly arguing with Dad about the profit booksellers and libraries made out of *their* hard-earned royalties. Secretary indeed, such luxuries belonged exclusively to the best-selling breed, the sex-and-violence boys.

Lady Ester said: 'Would—er, would twenty pounds a week be enough?'

'Oh, yes,' I said eagerly, and she sighed and gave a tiny smile.

'Then you'll do it—I'm so glad,' she beamed on me. 'My writer friend is Marie Hebburn.' She waited and I murmured politely, embarrassed that the name meant nothing to me. 'Her brother is Adam Hebburn—the painter.'

Again I looked blank, managed just in time to remember: 'Of course, the portrait in the hall.'

Lady Ester nodded. 'The Hebburns are a charming couple, absolutely charming. They live at Whitton Sands. A darling old house which used to be a smuggler's inn.'

Whitton Sands. If the money had given me cause for hesitation, the magic name 'Whitton Sands' would have been all the persuasion I needed. My absurd pulse raced, two weeks fully paid, to explore the Abbey—maybe a chance to meet my Horseman again. What a staggering coincidence, I thought. What marvellous luck.

As Lady Ester walked through the great hall with me I paused to look at Hector's portrait with new eyes. 'We watched *Sunrise on Avalon*

56

on television,' I said. 'It was super. He was a wonderful actor, wasn't he? I 'm sorry I missed seeing him. You must feel very proud to have such a genius in the family.'

Her eyes slid nervously to the painting and back again to me. 'Well, I don't have television,' she said and I was acutely aware of her abrupt change of subject. Probably she got wary of being pumped for inside information about her infamous nephew. 'Now you will remember our little arrangement. You won't let me down, will you, dear? Marie is depending on you ...'

The eyes of Hector Pleys followed me out. I could almost hear the beautiful voice ... Parking Mini near the drive, I decided to visit the grave of one of Britain's greatest actors.

Fog was rising from the river as I walked towards the graveyard. The wind blew suddenly cold and the sun stopped shining. Along the wooded path it was dark and autumnal, with last year's fallen leaves rustling like dead footfalls behind me.

Among the long-dead Pleys, on a raised plinth, a white marble figure lay. I walked round it, hushed and reverent, although there wouldn't be much left there after fifteen years. How awful to be dead—and I hurried away from my morbid imaginings, haunted by a strange feeling of sadness, of regret.

After that film, and the portrait in Pleys Castle. I felt I knew the dead man, with the suddenness, the intimacy, that kids 'feel' for their favourite pop stars. How I had laughed at Lucy, years ago, with her L.P.s, her scrapbooks, her sighs. Yet here I was with a quite inexplicable aching void, feeling cheated and bereft—that I would go anywhere to see this man who would be well past fifty if he were alive today.

Strange, it was as if I had been all ice inside until Charlie died. Marriage to me, a sentimental sexless cuddle in romantic firelight, my mind unable or unwilling to contemplate its ultimate conclusion of passion and abandoned desire. What had happened to me? Here I was looking fondly at Warren, shedding tears over the television demise of Hector Pleys as Arthur.

I didn't fool myself. The one to blame for this extraordinary awakening of my senses was the Horseman at Ninespears Crag. With some strange magic he had broken into my sleeping beauty world and unleashed the inhibitions that bound me faster than a magician's evil spell.

Whitton Sands. What luck. I drove out of the gates of Pleys Castle, chirping inside with delight. Perhaps I'd see him again. What an *amazing* stroke of gorgeous *super* luck.

Or so I thought. For when I reached Corham, although the tempo of life seemed unchanged, the people I loved the same, I returned as a female Rip Van Winkle driving through the little town.

In that hour at Pleys Castle, all unknowing, time had already moved on. My home in the Cloisters, everything dear and familiar to me, were already part of the past.

CHAPTER 3

I was wrong about everything. I thought I knew the exact reaction of my very predictable parents. Dad would be huffy, insist it was too lonely for a girl at Whitton Sands, and demand suspiciously:

'What are these people like, anyway?' And when I said: 'She's a writer, he paints,' Dad would say: 'Writers never pay their bills and painters aren't much catch these days' (meaning that they were dangerous to women's morals). And, of course, Mum would say: 'I hope they remember to feed you and that the beds are all aired.'

I put Mini in the garage and went into the house to tell them the news. I expected protest, fuss, long discussions about whether I was doing the right thing—and to be asked umpteen times a day: 'It *is* just two weeks—isn't it?'

I was in for a shock. Dad gave his great hearty guffaw, Mum kissed me and said: 'How marvellous. We're so glad for you, Julie.'

'Marie Hebburn the writer,' said Dad. 'Aye, that's a great chance for you.'

'It's only a couple of weeks,' I said apologetically. 'The autumn books are just coming into the shop, Dad. I promise to be back before they're in full flood.'

Dad shook his head. 'Don't worry, lass, don't worry. If we get busy your mum will give me a hand. Won't you, May?'

Mum smiled. 'I'd love that, Dick.' My eyes widened. Such appearances belonged to rare domestic crises, for Mum was convinced that without her constant presence in the kitchen at home Dad and I would starve to death.

'You deserve a break,' said Dad. And the whole scene between them, from Dad's arm on Mum's shoulder and her bright smile, looked suspiciously rehearsed. They were such appalling actors that I wondered if my new 'job' was such a surprise to them. Was this the reason why their weekly visit to Dad's folk in South Shields had been mysteriously cancelled? They were the only kin I had. Mum was an orphan, her only relative a much younger cousin, Jean, remembered by a fading photo among Mum's mementoes of the past and a yearly Christmas card from Canada.

Why the secrecy over my temporary job as

secretary to Marie Hebburn? We were a gossipy family who mulled over the smallest details of domesticity, and such behaviour was completely out of character. Besides, if Lady Ester *had* approached them first, they would have been bursting with excitement about it.

'Adam Hebburn, the artist. Remember that famous painting, May? The one you liked a few years ago?'

'Hector Pleys as King Arthur?' said Mum, frowning over her knitting as if nothing out of the ordinary had happened.

'No, no. The other one. He got an award for it. It had a funny title—oh, you must remember. It was in all the magazines. Famous as that green Chinese lass, for a while. Now, what *was* it called?'

'Er, "The Enchantress",' said Mum triumphantly. Dad shook his head. 'Yes, it was. I remember it perfectly, Dick. A girl's face looking out of autumn leaves, all lovely colours they were. Only you didn't see the girl at all until you looked closely. She looked like part of the scene. One of those surrealistic things. I'm sure it was "The Enchantress".'

And while Dad continued to say it wasn't, Mum went on about this picture with great knowledge and enthusiasm. Which was sur-

62

prising, considering she usually claimed her taste in art had been cultivated on: 'The Laughing Cavalier', 'The Boyhood of Raleigh', and 'When Did You Last See Your Father?', prints collected by Grandfather saving cigarette cards in her young day.

Next day Mum packed my suitcase, as if I were away to the Arctic on a two-year geological survey, instead of two weeks forty miles away. Dad was hoping Adam Hebburn might teach me something about art, and Mum, chatting to friends on the telephone, already basking in the vicarious glory of a daughter who hob-nobs with the famous.

Warren took me over to the farm to tell Mrs Browne. Ashamed, I dreaded visits to her these days. She still cried a lot about Charlie and hugged me tearfully when we parted. I stood there unable to shed a tear, because after those first beastly weeks when Charlie died I seemed to have cried myself out.

'It's the best thing for you, Julie love,' she said. 'You must miss Charlie so much. You'd have been married three months now—I'm always thinking about it.' She took out a hanky, dabbed her eyes. 'Oh dear ...'

Warren, lurking in the background, watched his mother anxiously. Doleful and embarrassed, as always, by displays of feminine emotions.

'Take care of her, Warren love,' she said, and waved to us both as we went back down the farm road. The dear familiar road I had known—and with it the Browne boys—all my life.

Charlie and I were inseparable as children. Never between us the sex hatred of under-twelves. As teenagers our marriage seemed foreordained—the happy ending for childhood sweethearts.

Once, rebelling against its very inevitability, longing for something emotionally stronger than lifelong comradeship—but a coward when it came to telling Charlie so—I escaped. To a bleak miserable job in an office in Grey Street, Newcastle. It wasn't far enough to run—I should have gone further. Charlie was at Durham University and came through every weekend. My digs were hateful, with awful food and a prying landlady. Soon Charlie and I were seeing more of each other than ever we did in Corham.

He persuaded me to resign and confident that 'rebellion' had got discontent out of my system, I went back home and we announced our engagement to the delighted families. Secret-ly, I knew I shouldn't have been a weak fool and sorry for myself. Suddenly I was sure this decision would bring neither of us happiness. Least of all Charlie.

Now, like his brother, Warren waited on the sidelines, like a good-natured vulture, to pick up the pieces of my broken life. At the bus station grumbling, slightly ferocious, he said: 'Why do you have to go away there, anyway?' He was turning possessive too, telling me: 'We worry about you,' when I protested. As if I had been married to Charlie instead of only engaged, and this gave Warren some kind of tribal rights over me.

The situation developing with Warren made me glad to go. He had a keen sense of property. I remember him as a child defending everything he owned with tooth, claw and pugnacious chin. Now I saw the adult version of the same expressions. Like those early toys, I had been marked down as his own. Misgivings about what he called 'our friendship' I had in plenty. And before this tirade on what I still considered *my* business to go where I damned well pleased —two weeks or two years—I firmly dug in my heels.

'Girls have been known to take jobs out of their home towns before. Sometimes they even emigrate and fly all alone in aeroplanes to

Canada, like Mum's cousin did.' But sarcasm was lost on Warren, who merely shuddered and kissed my mouth, warmly ignoring the cheek I primly offered in good fellowship. The parents said they weren't coming to see me off, but did. Warren was exceptionally pleased that they were in time to witness the tender scene of our leave-taking, seeing himself as 'one of the family', the role dearest to his heart especially in public places. The resulting embarrassment all round turned it into one of those awful station partings from a bad film about World War II, full of poignant silences, stiff upper lips, with everything said except goodbye.

The bus moved off. Hearty waves were exchanged. Why on earth the sad faces? My practical down-to-earth mum and dad behaving like Ancient Greek parents seeing a beloved child off to be the Minotaur's breakfast. A horrid simile, I thought, and taking a seat thoughtfully, I concentrated on the way ahead.

We left the main road and danced down some pretty lanes, meandering in a bonny valley, prim and daintily spread as a Victorian posy, tied with a blue ribbon of river, the Tyne. At this point the Tyne had never heard of industry and had never had its waters sullied by more than a cow with sore feet. Abruptly we began to climb, higher and higher, to where Nine-spears Crag held the horizon of a dark and savage-looking moor, broodily waiting for us.

It didn't scare me. I watched it grow larger, nearer, enjoying the glowing afternoon. There was nothing in this tranquil scene to call up that night of mist, sinister Peel Tower and ghostly Horseman.

Idly, I wondered if Marie Hebburn would satisfy my curiosity about the Hermit and if I would ever again see my twentieth-century knight who had ridden out of the mist, falcon on fist, to rescue a maid in a Mini. I thought of the power and majesty of his face, born clear out of its time. A medieval face ... Would I see him again? Surely, if he were part of life at Whitton Sands, which, according to Dad, was half the size of Corham.

'A Northumbrian fishing village. Once famous for kippers,' said the guide-book. 'A hundred years ago its fame lay in smuggling and wrecking. The cliffs are still full of caves, relics of the old hideaways ...'

If I didn't meet the Horseman—my main reason for taking this job with Marie Hebburn—I'd be bitterly disappointed. You'll probably be more disappointed when you see him in daylight, I told myself. He'll be forty-five and grey, a bluff jovial farmer with a plump homely wife and teenage children ...

I sighed. Warren was right when he said: 'You dream too much, Julie. You'd build romance out of a stone dyke—turn it into a giant's castle ...'

And Lucy had me taped too. She'd laugh and say: 'Julie, you missed your chance. You should have been an actress—you make drama out of everything. You think men are romantic when they're just, well, sexy ... You build great dreams around everyone you meet, see great friendships ahead. Then you're disappointed and angry with *them*—feeling they've let *you* down by not living up to the impossible standards *you've* invented for them.'

'Whitton Sands? Down the road there,' said the bus conductress. Swinging my suitcase, excited and relieved to be away from my miserable thoughts, I walked down the road, and noticed with joy there was the very ditch where I left Mini. On my left a loftly sunlit hill, Ninespears Crag, held the centre of the stage.

It was all so different today, thank heaven. With birdsong and sunshine a setting for rustic romance. How on earth had this tranquil spot ever seemed eerie, or scary? The tree-lined road dipped sharply down to a prospect of distant red roofs, perched above the blue glitter of the sea. A stiffish breeze rustled leaves on trees, still soft and green, no longer witch-like, frightening shadows.

On the sea an island floated. Far-off and misty, with the shape of a castle lifted from some fairy-tale. Holy Island.

Holy Island. Even here I couldn't escape memories of Charlie. Two summers ago we stayed there for a weekend. Eating lobster salads, walking to Lindisfarne Priory in a high wind. And quarrelling—as usual. All because I turned sulky when he insisted we should get married that autumn.

I walked down the road slower now, my step not quite so light, for the day's beauty had changed, curdled into pity and pain for Charlie, for whom all the seasons now bloomed and faded in vain. And conscience, a wild creature refusing to be neatly trapped in any cage, cried out: 'If you hadn't quarrelled he would never have gone out and got killed ...' Common sense pleaded: 'Another motor-bike, another day. He always drove too fast ... Other people warned him ...' To which conscience screamed: 'It was *your* fault, all your fault ...'

I stopped, tried to recapture my fine sense of adventure. But it was no use. There was heavy lead in my heart with the magic prettiness of Whitton Sands turned to ashes as I fled from the strange and bitter world of 'Might-have-been.'

By daylight Whitton Peel wasn't sinister at all. Just a lonely grey tower, silent among tall trees. If I go and knock at the door, I thought, today it'll be opened by a large red-faced jolly woman eager to be friendly. Behind her, the kitchen neat and homely with pots bubbling and smells of baking.

The Peel was still some distance away when a signpost pointing down to the right indicated: 'Whitton Sands Harbour and Priory'. I followed the pebbly road which branched off again, a sandy track up a steep whin-covered hill, concealing all but the skeleton of Whitton Priory's famous Norman arch, pointing into the sky like the wishbone of some prehistoric monster.

Clustered near the harbour were dilapidated sheds, carrying faded trade names. Broken windows and roofs suggested Whitton Sands hadn't contributed very much to home industry this side of 1900. The pebbled beach was lapped by a tiny frill of lace—the incoming tide. Far out of its reach, lobster pots and rust-coloured nets crouched against the harbour wall and discarded boats moored upside down, shabby, paintless, suggested an obsolete race of crustaceans.

Near some parked cars a few couples walked arm-in-arm along the pier, slowly, stopping to look at the sea, like elderly invalids enjoying a break in bad weather. Above the harbour wall, nestling into the cliffside, a street of whitewashed cottages, one converted into an inn: the Whitton Arms, with a very small card in its window advertising Bed and Breakfast. It was too small to have been the famous smuggler's inn. There was nothing worthy in size of Priory House, either, none of the houses distinguished by names or numbers. I strolled along, waiting hopefully for someone, sent by Miss Hebburn to meet me.

As the minutes passed, I realised with dismay that Mum's forebodings were probably right. In an artist's house everyone would be disorganised, their enriched creative temperaments beyond the prosaic conventions of meeting buses or eating regular meals.

The couples had finished their walks and the pier was now deserted but for one man who sat on a barrel staring moodily out to sea. If he was waiting for me, he wasn't doing a very efficient job. As I walked towards him—at least he could tell me the way to the Hebburns—I noticed he was very handsome in profile, with dark curly hair and sideburns. The kind of profile that needs a sailor's gold ear-ring, above navy sweater and jeans. Handsome but rather frail, he suggested a seagoing Lord Byron, waiting for inspiration.

'Excuse me, can you tell me ...' He turned and my words died in a flurry of embarrassment '... the way—er—to Priory House?'

Eyes sadly too pale for the dark face raked over and dismissed me. 'You should have stayed on the Main Road ... ignored the signpost to the harbour ... the house is up there opposite.'

I gave a sigh of relief. There was no recognition. Mumbling thanks, I walked away, not having understood a word he said, and too embarrassed to ask him to repeat the directions. Or he might remember where we had met before.

I walked quickly towards the Whitton Arms. When I looked back he wasn't watching me. I had ceased to exist, one among several hundred girls he had made a pass at in his time, no doubt ... A medical student, and very drunk, at the University Athletic Ball, he had been flirting with me all evening. Finally Charlie hit him.

'What did you do that for, for heaven's sake?'
I asked.

'I'm fussy about who my girl necks with. Everybody knows—'(the name was forgotten), 'and his reputation,' said Charlie.

'Maybe everybody does, but I don't. And for your information I wasn't necking with him.' Later I learned he came from a wealthy New-castle family and ruined a brilliant career in a rather nasty drug scandal. Presumably he had found some quiet niche in Whitton Sands. I hoped so.

Inside the Whitton Arms, all romance of creaking sign and ancient whitewashed cottage died, in an onslaught of ocelot plastic, neon lighting and juke-box stridenly pleading for 'Love, love, love ...' With two hours until open-ing time, its insistence seemed indecently eager.

Wiping the counter and apparently deaf to the din, was a tall burly man with a pugilist's nose and hair so patently black it did not com-pute with a tired seamed face that must have seen sixty summers.

I asked for directions to Priory House, please.

'Came on the bus, did ye? Aye, then ye should have stayed on the main road and paid no attention to the signpost.' He pointed through the window. 'Thon's yer road up there'

—a white ribbon toiled steeply upwards and vanished over the hill. 'I dare say ye could take the old smugglers' road up the cliff—the old Brandy Road—it's naught but a track up the old cliff-face, but quicker than going t'other way round ...' He grinned, tiny pebble-black eyes crawling all over me. 'Priory House, eh?' And he chuckled rather nastily as if I'd told him a dirty joke. As I said a polite but chilly thanks and walked away, he shouted: 'Hey, want to leave your case? We'll send it up later.'

'No, thanks. It isn't heavy.'

The young man on the barrel had disappeared and the pier, devoid of sunshine, was empty. A stiff wind blew in from the sea and, trying to preserve my morning's hair-set, I took out the white headscarf and tied it carefully as I walked up the sandy track at the foot of the cliff that the sheep had started long ago. With constant flurries of wind and sand, it still managed to be highly inadequate.

Here and there the firmer ground was pitted with horses' hoofmarks. Transferring my case from hand to hand as I climbed, I decided it would take an expert horseman to climb that vertical track. However, it must have been accomplished with regularity—and success—in the past, to earn itself the name of the

'Brandy Road'.

Heart hammering, breathing hard, I reached the top.

'Melanie.' I stopped, listened. Had I imagined a voice above the seagulls' lament? Doubtless it was the wind sighing across the wild moorland that stretched to the very edge of the cliffs. A bleak and bitter prospect. Lit now by a thin trickle of sunshine, stark light and darkened sky added to the curious desolation which typifies the Northumbrian moors. As though created by some strange giants in a forgotten world and abandoned like a child's game, before the breath of life had properly kindled.

Then I noticed the smoke. One perfunctory plume, rising from a hollow of trees straight ahead. The giants experimenting with soft, fertile things had gone mad with a paintbrush, scattering yellow of larch, orange of horse-chestnut, magenta of wild cherry, among the solid green. Perhaps in a fit of mutinous despair they tossed the moor's bitter edge over into the blue North Sea .... The cold North Sea—a ludicrous backdrop to a scene of heathered moor and crag, as if this week's *Lucia di Lammermoor* were being rehearsed against last week's *H.M.S. Pinafore*.

Wearily I transferred my case to the other hand, stretched out numbed fingers. I was feeling cross. Those trees were some distance away with only the track through the heather. I concluded that Adam Hebburn must be sadly lacking in manners—I saw him, grey, shambling and unshaven, wearing ancient flannels spattered with paint and cigarette ash cascading down the front of a sagging cardigan ...

'Melanie—Melanie ...' A flash of white wings, a scream of anger as a seagull disturbed hurtled downward to the sea, leaving his harsh cry echoing across the blighted landscape.

'Melanie—wait—wait.' And behind me up the track a young girl came half-running, half-stumbling, all bubbling excitement and laughter.

Two yards away from me she stopped, and in a voice of ashes said: 'It's not you at all. You're not Melanie.' Radiance faded from her face as she blinked at me short-sightedly from under the mane of long fairish hair.

'I thought you were someone else,' she mumbled, lip trembling on the edge of tears. Whoever Melanie was, she possessed strong magic to have transformed this ugly duckling into momentary illusion of swan. I felt awful—as if I had intentionally cheated her in

76

some way.

'I'm sorry,' she said, recovering. 'I don't have my glasses.'

'Don't apologise. I'm on my way to Priory House—is that it?'

She nodded absently. 'Yes, they're expecting you. You're not really like Melanie at all, you know. She has auburn hair and green eyes—but from a distance, that white headscarf ...' She paused, inspected me again. 'How did you know the short cut, anyway? Most people who go to Priory House go down the main road. It's just a step—couple of hundred yards.'

When I explained and told her, rather pointedly, that when there was no one to meet me, I asked directions at Whitton Arms.

'Didn't they tell you the old Brandy Road was dangerous? We don't like strangers coming up this way—you can see how shaky it is—and in bad weather there's a lot of subsidence, landslides and so forth. I expect that's why I thought you were Melanie,' she added crossly. 'She always came this way from Whitton Sands, weather never bothered her. She even rode up it—nothing frightened her. She was fascinated by danger.' And she began to lope away across the heather towards the house.

Floundering behind her, I said: 'I'm sorry,'

sounding like a mourner offering condolences at a funeral. 'Who's Melanie?'

'Hmm?' said the girl absently. 'I'm Diane Scales. Aunt Marie's expecting you.' One of the family, just my luck to start off on the wrong foot. She stopped, looked back longingly towards the way we had come. As if a further selection of girls in white headscarfs might appear, bearing the missing Melanie in their midst.

'I'm not really related, I just call them aunt and uncle. My father is vicar of St. Cuthbert's—down there by the harbour. Do you know Whitton Priory?' she asked proudly, pointing to the beautiful arch lingering by a distant rubble of unidentifiable stones. 'The pilgrims used to rest there on their way to Lindisfarne Priory—over there.'

A strange ship, permanently at anchor, Holy Island rested on the sea. There were other islands, smaller ones ...

'Is that Whitton Peel?' I asked pointing to the grey tower rising behind the hollow of trees. She said it was and I asked: 'Who lives there?'

She stared at me, said: 'Watch your nylons, it's a bit rough this way.' It was indeed. I was too preoccupied to play question and answer.

Finally we emerged over stile and dyke to a solid-looking sandstone house.

Square and business-like, two hundred years old, ivy climbed the front wall, suggesting mellowness and tranquillity within. We took a side path. Through the trees, a glimpse of other buildings. A horse whinnied ... 'That's Starlight. Stables and garage over there,' said Diane, and opening the back door: 'Excuse the kitchen.' Apology was inconsistent for that well-scrubbed floor, gleaming copper pans and horse-brasses, the smell of furniture polish, and pot plants blooming in chintz-curtained windows.

'I'll take you to your room.' Hall and stairs were oak-panelled. Open doors revealed rooms comfortably furnished and rather old-fashioned in taste. There were well-bred airs of mahogany, white paint and Persian rugs. I had expected a more venturesome taste in pictures. Some original 'Adam Hebburns' rather than the still-lifes and flowers, prints obtainable in any chain store across the country.

'Here we are ...' The room she ushered me into was enormous, a beautiful piece of Victoriana, from brass bedstead to Gog and Magog patiently contemplating infinity from the mantelpiece. The furniture was massive rosewood and the bed had an almost clinical whiteness in linen.

If this was the guest room then the Hebburns were doing me proud. There were two windows each with cushioned sill. The east-facing one looked down into a secluded rustic garden with a white wooden seat, and far beyond it to the sea. Through the other window to the north, the gaunt grey face of Whitton Peel stared down on us, overshadowed by the sombre Ninespear Crag. 'Wardrobe's full just now,' and eyeing my small case. 'Perhaps you can make do with this. Bathroom's at the end of the hall ...'

At the foot of the stairs a woman in a wheel-chair propelled herself across to meet me. My vision of Marie Hebburn as a dowdy middle-aged spinster, face twisted and pinched by suffering, collapsed before this porcelain beauty with the blonde curls, the wide-spaced blue eyes of a Botticelli angel.

Coming downstairs, smiling, I realised that if the shock I received by her appearance was pleasing, my impact on her, was quite the reverse. The light was behind me. Suddenly her eyes dilated, one hand flew to her throat and her hands tightened on the arms of the chair as if she wanted to leap out of it, run for cover. Fear—and something else. Hate. The hatred in those eyes rang a bell. I had seen eyes remarkably like them—and recently.

'This is Julie Marsden, Aunt Marie,' said Diane, coming from the kitchen.

With a frightened smile, Marie Hebburn took my hand in one that still trembled. And the silence after our mumbled 'how do you do' was broken by Diane's shaky laugh. Her stage whisper:

'I thought she was Melanie, too.'

At that moment the front door opened and the young man from the barrel on the pier burst in. Something had put him into a high old temper:

'What the devil's going on here?' he demanded. 'Marie—why wasn't I told?'

Then he saw me.

CHAPTER 4

The young man with the familiar face had a name I remembered vaguely.

'Dr. Philip Riche.' After introducing us Marie said rather imperiously: 'I'm busy—as you can see, Phil. Will it do later? Come along, Miss Marsden.' He bowed to us with a kind of old-fashioned grace and wheeled her chair into the study.

'Thank you, dear,' she said, dismissing him. Then to me: 'May I call you Julie?'

I said of course and with a briskness of manner rarely associated with porcelain ladies she told me quickly about the job in hand. 'I need an index, a bibliography—some cross-references. It's all rather tedious, I'm afraid, and I'm such a muddle-head,' she added with an apologetic smile.

I thought she might be many things, but muddle-head was not one of them.

'I gather you can be spared for two weeks, Julie. Lady Ester thinks highly of you—she's such a dear, getting a bit vague, of course, she's nearly eighty. But still very much the grand lady of the manor, don't you think?' I agreed and she was obviously pleased.

'Makes it her business to know everything about everybody. Bosses all her friends—and we love it. I envy you Corham, such a heavenly place. I used to be mad about Roman history—planned a book about Hadrian's Wall—used to come to Corham quite often to the Roman museum. Then—this,' she indicated the wheel-chair. 'So now the best I can manage is wild flowers ...'

On the desk the telephone rang. She carried on half a minute's monosyllabic conversation then hung up. 'My brother Adam. He sent his apologies. Been delayed in Berwick on business overnight. Well, I have some notes to make—perhaps after dinner? If you're not too tired?' As I reached the door she said: 'Ask Diane if there's any quarto typing paper in the house.'

I found Diane in the kitchen peeling potatoes.

'There'll be some in Uncle Adam's studio,' she said shortly. We went upstairs, down the corridor where a small flight of stairs led into a room with a ceiling almost entirely glass.

'What a beautiful room,' I said, and sniffed the air. Where was the smell of turps and linseed? Where was the chaos of the working artist? Brushes soaking, half-finished paintings? An easel and a few canvases turned their faces against one wall.

Either Adam Hebburn was a formidably tidy man or it was long since this room had been used each day. A couple of Victorian chairs with withered upholstery had found their way in, and an old-fashioned bird perch, the kind parrot owners have, lolled in one corner, adding a sense of desolation ...

'Here's your paper.' I left her and walked back along the corridor past the family's bedrooms, where female curiosity was obligingly appeased by doors all open on sunny south-facing rooms, not one with the elegance, the dramatic view, of mine. Glad to be alone for a while, I closed the door, feeling strangely lost and homesick. Where had my fine sense of adventure gone? I decided bare arms accounted for that sudden feeling of chill and decided to change into a skirt and sweater.

Suddenly I found the room ablaze with colour ...

Absent-mindedly I had opened the wardrobe door. It was crammed with clothes. Women's clothes. Jewelled cocktail dresses, evening gowns, furs and velvets. Even a perfunctory glance showed rich elegance, obvious expense. On a shelf underneath, innumerable shoes waited neatly in pairs. To dance, to dine, to walk, to ride ...

In guilty haste I closed the door, but the subtle perfume released from the captive clothes remained. In a panic I threw open the window as downstairs someone rang the bell for dinner.

Dr. Philip Riche was there. Surprisingly civilised by lounge suit and tie, his greeting was courteous.

'Congratulations on a splendid casserole,' said Marie to Diane, who blushed with pleasure when I added my compliments. Philip said nothing, but behaved in a manner befitting the host, attentive to my comfort, searching in the sideboard for an extra glass-mat, seeing to my wine.

'Did Diane tell you this was once a smugglers' inn?' said Marie, making conversation. 'Long ago, of course, before it was considered smart to have a seaside cottage for weekends— with cocktails and television just within reach at the local inn.'

'The Whitton Arms looks new and expensive. I don't care too much for their jungly theme,' I said, helping her out.

'All that imitation ocelot is a bit much, isn't

it?' she said.

'Have you been to Whitton Sands before?' asked Philip.

'Not really. Apart from getting lost in mist a couple of weeks ago. I didn't know about Priory House then. Tried to get help at the Peel Tower. Does anyone live there?' I asked casually, looking up from my cheese and biscuits.

Coffee-cups raised, three pairs of eyes watched me. Intently, like starving pussy-cats outside a mousehole. Quick imploring looks were exchanged.

'Just a hermit,' said Marie, her voice curiously flat. 'Diane tells me you came up the old Brandy Road. It's fairly steep to imagine ponies staggering under loads of contraband ...'

'Do you know, Miss Marsden,' said Diane, 'there's supposed to be a secret passage, right underneath us, leading to a cave on the shore. And down in the cellar you can actually hear the sea at high tide. Like listening to a sea-shell ...'

'If you'll excuse me,' said Philip, his amused but weary glance in Diane's direction indicating that he had heard it all before. 'I expect I'll be seeing Miss Marsden later,' he added with a slight smile in my direction.

'Do call her Julie,' said Marie. 'And isn't it

nice that she's going to work for us?'

'Us?' Philip raised a mocking eyebrow. 'Well, it'll be the first time any of "us" were ever included in Adam's arrangements.' As he walked behind my chair, he put a hand on my shoulder. 'I hope all this talk of smugglers won't frighten you away. Remember the old warning: "Watch the wall, my darling, as the gentlemen go by".'

I turned with a polite smile, but his face was serious and rather sad.

Marie apparently felt some need to apologise for the heavy silence that followed his departure: 'You must forgive Philip leaving us so abruptly. He is so overworked in his practise.' And to Diane, who snorted rudely at this remark, she added: 'This is Uncle Adam's house, you know.'

There was a note of warning, something else, too, that had been bothering me. *I* had understood from Lady Ester Pleys that Marie Hebburn had negotiated my services as *her* secretary. But Philip had referred to 'Adam's arrangements'.

'I'll get my notes,' said Marie hurriedly. 'No, no, please—finish your coffee.'

Diane giggled nervously when we were alone. 'Don't mind Philip. He's a bit on edge these days.' A moment later she added: 'He doesn't like people much.'

'His patients must find him trying,' I said.

'Patients?' echoed Diana, as if it was a word completely new to her. Looking startled, she managed a tiny laugh: 'O-oh, patients hardly rank as people where Phil's concerned. People are o-u-t.'

'Has he found something to take their place?' I asked.

'We-ll,' she said, eyeing me doubtfully, 'he does like animals,' she added triumphantly. 'He loves ...' And quite suddenly her voice trailed off.

I turned round. Marie had wheeled herself silently back into the room with a sheaf of papers on her knee. There was a long silence broken when she said, studying quiet tensionless hands: 'He loves horses, doesn't he, dear, isn't that what you were saying?'

Diana gave a sigh of relief. 'Oh yes. Melanie has this horse and Philip is the only one who can really ride him. Do you ride, Miss Marsden? Oh pity, you'd love Thunder—even if he is a devil ...'

'Could we go into the study?' interrupted Marie, a bright smiling mouth belied by strange haunted eyes. 'I have some things ready now.'

Closing the door behind us, she said, as if excusing Diane, 'At fifteen, one is madly enthusiastic about everything. When one gets older one remembers youth as a time when all the days were sunny. Everything was better—times, clothes, weather.' She smiled. 'One forgets that even the young—and fit—can be unhappy too.'

Later when I had taken notes of what she required she said: 'I hope you'll be happy with us.' When I said I was sure to be, she nodded. 'I realise how bad it's been for you, Julie. Lady Ester told me—the Brownes were so well thought of—farmed in Corham for generations, haven't they? I believe there's a nice policeman brother—Wilson?' And she gave me a look that tried sternly not to be arch.

'No, Warren ...' Suddenly I was telling her about Warren, wondering whether I should get involved with him.

'Well, why not? There's nothing wrong with marrying for liking and respect, as long as *you* don't pretend to yourself that this is really love. That's just asking for trouble to start, for disillusions ...'

I went into the kitchen and made coffee. 'Not for me, I wouldn't sleep a wink,' said Marie. 'Good night, Julie.' I decided I liked her very much. There was a feeling of some shared wave-length. Perhaps it was an air of frailty that gave her a deceptive youthfulness and brought her closer to my own generation.

As I went upstairs the door of my bedroom was rattling furiously. Frantically, as if someone trapped inside was trying to escape ...

I discovered the reason soon enough. The tranquil evening had died under a harsh east wind and through the open window dead leaves, blown in from the trees in the sunken garden, were scattered everywhere.

Gathering them up, I decided I was over-imaginative about the odd behaviour of the people at Priory House and wrote a letter of considerable length and reassurance to Lucy.

My head had barely touched the pillow when the wraith of perfume returned ... Furiously, I closed my eyes, but sleep would be neither threatened nor cajoled. The deep boom of the sea. It must be high tide, for it sounded oppressively near, as if it stretched out to touch the garden ... Its monotonous sound became another presence, like another heart-beat in the bed beside me. Suddenly the nor'easter blowing at the window, shaking the trees, was a red-headed girl, running, crying, her dress torn and muddied. Melanie, Melanie, Melanie ...

I sat up in bed, wide-awake, and decided uncharitably that this magnificent room was unused by the family simply because it was noisy, restless, and on stormy nights sleep would be quite impossible.

I wondered to whom clothes and perfume belonged. Not Marie somehow. The missing Melanie, of course. Her room with clothes and shoes, all neat and orderly awaiting her return. From where?

Twelve was striking on the hall clock as I went cautiously downstairs. All those bookshelves in the study must have something I could read. I'd been a fool to come with neither books nor the sleeping pills, so much a necessity of my life since Charlie's death.

A thread of light gleamed under Marie's door opposite the study. So someone else kept late hours. With a paperback of short stories I was leaving again when Marie's door opened. In a panic I half-closed the study door, furiously embarrassed at meeting my new employer while patrolling the house at midnight in my dressing-gown. Snooping was the word that came most readily to mind.

There were voices. Philip Riche was there, leaning over her chair. He kissed her. 'Darling, you must go,' she said, 'you really must ...'

The words belied by the wistful radiance of her face.

'Damn it all, Marie, when can we be together? Why the devil don't you defy him? We can get married—whenever you like. I'll tell you one thing—I'm bloody sick of having to creep about to see you secretly, as if you were under age or something.'

'Listen—I thought I heard a car. Listen.' She sounded terrified.

'It isn't coming here. And even if it were ... Damn him. I don't care. What business is it of his? I know I'm young, I haven't much to offer. But I do love you.'

'Phil dear, you know perfectly well why he objects to you. I don't see that you can blame him ...'

'Oh, that other damned nonsense. It was over before it began almost. And you've forgiven me—you're the one who suffered—all this ... We all make mistakes. Besides, she'll never come back, you must realise that. It's all over, finished.'

'Is it, Phil? Is it really finished? I'd like to believe it but I can't. There are too many shadows—even this girl. No, Phil my dear, nothing is ever really finished here. It can't ever be. *While he is still alive ...*'

I knew by her voice that she was crying. I heard the chair being wheeled back into the study, Philip saying: 'Let me stay ... let me stay tonight.' His voice sounded harsh, broken, as the door closed behind them.

I crept upstairs, strangely touched by the tender scene I had witnessed. Presumably Dr. Philip Riche with a practice in Whitton Peel was a far cry from the medical student with a fast reputation. But what could this woman, invalid, bookish, expect from such an alliance with an active, virile man more than ten years her junior. Perhaps she had money. I was ashamed of the thought, against my will recalling old university scandals when his family disowned him.

'How uncharitable,' said conscience, 'that was long ago.'

I didn't sleep comfortably that night, for more reasons than being in a strange bed. What kind of ogre was Adam Hebburn that the Porcelain Beauty wanted her brother dead?

'Nothing is ever really finished here ... while he is still alive.'

I shivered at the memory of those words, recognising that this was no hysterical statement, but one with the ring of an oft-discussed and accepted fact.

Obviously Adam opposed his sister's wish to marry Philip Riche. But why? If they loved each other, for in her tragic circumstances it was doubtful if many offers of marriage would come her way? That 'other damned nonsense' where Marie had suffered could only be referring to the missing Melanie, whom Philip was certain would 'never come back'.

What else had Marie said? Something about 'too many shadows—even this girl'. I felt suddenly cold. That must be me. But what had I to do with their lives? How could my brief stay at Priory House as Marie's secretary be connected with whatever drama they were enacting? It was dawn when I fell asleep feeling sorry for the poor lovers. Hateful, cruel monster, that was Adam Hebburn right enough. I wished I didn't have to meet him ...

I awoke to a serene and tranquil morning, after a half-remembered sinister dream about Melanie and this room packed with her clothes, smelling still of her perfume ... I looked out of the window. Only some freshly fallen leaves, the balding trees in the sunken garden gave evidence of the earlier storm. The air was crisp and clean, and somewhere nearby a horse neighed in joyous recognition ... Starlight greeted the day's first visitor to his stable.

After a solitary do-it-yourself breakfast in the kitchen I started work on the notes Marie had left. Anxious to impress with speed and efficiency I handed them to her at lunch.

'How marvellous,' she said, 'this would have taken me days to write out.' Diane served us eggs benedict and Marie told me: 'She wants to study domestic science. Her father is a widower, and the vicarage really needs a woman's touch. We share a daily, Mrs Miles ...'

Later she said: 'What a pity I haven't anything else ready for you to type. It's such a lovely day, why not take the chance of seeing the Priory. On a windy day it can be most unpleasant up there on the cliffs ...' Although she carried on a smiling conversation, her eyes were haggard, her mind elsewere. On Philip, no doubt.

I tidied my desk, covered the typewriter and wondered where this room, with its well-worn scratched oak panelling, had fitted into the old inn—what dramas of blood and death, of excise men and smugglers had been witnessed by these long silent walls ...

I went into the garden with its lively fragment of stream, the kind that appears and disappears at will on the savage wild moors. In the sunken garden visible from both study and my bedroom above, the trees chosen for their variety of colour blazed in full splendour—before an empty seat. It seemed a shame not to please them with admiration, so I sat down enjoying the beauty of it all, with only the starlings' peevish argument over a crust of bread, the harsh clear notes of a blackbird's warning cry to break the spell.

A leaf, blood-red, fluttered down. I caught it, marvelling at the simple perfection. The sun was sinking, now the house stood sharply etched in light and shade, the more polished outline of long ago belonging to smugglers, highwaymen.

A footfall. My own heart-beat noisy as the blackbird above my head, as a curly male head disappeared into the front door. It wasn't russet, that was an illusion of the light. It was Philip again.

And all the troubles, all the tantalising fragments of last night, destroyed my serenity. I got up, walked quickly out of the garden, feeling like an idiot. Always, searching, searching ... Mad, mad woman, to fall in love with a ghost ...

There was disappointingly little Priory left to see. Then surprisingly, set into four-feet-thick stone wall, a Crusader and his lady slept, hand in hand with a tiny dog curled at their feet. The lady on the outside had suffered more from the elements, her features, like the tombstones alongside, almost obliterated by wind and weather.

I went forward, took a closer look at the Crusader. Under the helmet, high cheekbones in a fighter's face—hard, but with an unexpectedly gentle mouth. Squinting down at him, suddenly the nape of my neck tingled. I had seen a face like that before. And not too long ago ...

The search for my lost love was over. My Horseman—so I *had* seen a ghost that night. The great horse, the falcon, none of them was real ... I touched his cheek, his mouth. Oh, my long lost love, I could search the world and never find you now. Dead for eight hundred years ...

My cheeks were wet with tears. I couldn't stay here, by the grave of my long-dead love ... The great ruined arch, its shadow deepening, the stone warm under my hand as the day they laid him in his tomb.

Seagulls cried, swooped over the sea. Rooks rose high over Priory House, soared into the air filling it with anger.

I turned and ran. Half-blinded by my tears,

I screamed, for my headlong flight took me straight to him. Straight to my russet-haired ghost, out of the tomb where he should have been lying. Asleep. At peace.

Straight into his arms ...

CHAPTER 5

Straight into his arms ... Arms of flesh and blood and muscle that put a stop to my headlong flight.

I must have screamed again and frightened him. God knows which of us was more startled by the encounter. As of watching from far off, I saw him step back, hold me at arm's length, lips drawn back over clenched teeth. Then the scene came to life like a film still suddenly animated.

My Horseman was alive. And in a kind of crazy drunken joy I felt all time rolled into one delicious moment of existence, with seagulls soaring above our heads and the wild waves beating on the rocks far below the ruined Priory. In that moment I was born. Burningly alive as I had never been before. Every single hair on my head tingled, right down to my toenails I was conscious of each fibre as I looked at the living man who held my arms.

His eyes were so near I could see the darker

shades of blue radiating from the black pupil, a microscopic world. I could feel his breath, see it hold for a moment, then vanish like small gossamer clouds on the heavy air.

'Oops,' he said. He was real. Capable of love and warm kisses ... Oops, indeed. Ghosts don't say oops. Nor do they wear modern raincoats. Under the pulled-up collar a brilliant glimpse of white shirt, dark tie, lounge suit. The air of comfortable elegance and clothes donned hastily, carelessly, by a man who nevertheless has inborn style and who probably managed to look quite breath-taking should the occasion demand it. There was even a drift of aftershave lotion.

'You must be Julie Marsden,' he said. I was charmed—nobody but my family and close friends ever called me Julie. But the further significance of such intimacy at first meeting was lost on me under the arch at Whitton Priory.

'For a moment I thought I was seeing things—you swooping down at me like a great bird.' He handed me a handkerchief. 'Dry your eyes. Go on, it's clean.'

I touched my face and found it wet with tears. I felt idiotic, crying because I was happy. Happy in the unexpected sheer joy of being in love. Not with a Crusader's ghost, conjured up

100

by a misty night on Ninespears Crag, but with a man capable of arousing me to emotional heights undreamed of ... Obediently I dried my eyes.

'The wind up here makes my eyes stream too,' he said sympathetically. But there was no wind today, bless his heart. 'I'm Adam Hebburn,' he added, holding out his hand.

Adam Hebburn the Ogre, with the porcelain-pretty sister and her secret lover, both of them longing for him to be dead? It wasn't possible.

'You look surprised,' he said.

'Well,' I said hastily, 'I expected a famous artist to be older.'

'You're very flattering, ma'am.' He gave a little bow. 'Famous. My, that was long ago. You must have been in the cradle then.' And he laughed, looking at me sideways, teasing.

'Nonsense, Adam Hebburn is a household word. Like D'Oyly John or Peter Scott. Everyone knows you ...'

'Maybe they did once,' he shrugged. 'But times have changed. I'm rather *passé* in the fashionable art world. Now only tired old men with lots of money want me to paint their ugly mistresses. Or city councillors who want to buy a few feet of immortality on the Town House walls.' He sighed. 'I haven't had a gimmick in umpteen years, you know. I can't keep up with pop art—I want more than riding bicycles through pots of paints and all that lark, or collages made from greasy newspapers straight off the fish-and-chip supper. I'm just an old-fashioned painter who likes his sitters attractive, striking or essentially paintable, to have faces preferably with two eyes, a nose and mouth and, please God, all of those in the conventional places.'

As he talked I watched him, stunned that this was *the* Adam Hebburn. Where was my elderly artist with beard, sparse grey hair and dandruff? Biting a pipe between ill-fitting dentures or, at best, long-discoloured yellow teeth like an ancient horse. Slovenly, grumpy too, my mind had said, addicted to berets, drooping cardigans and thick grey flannels—not to mention the Bottle. My eyes widened, Adam Hebburn, this vital-looking man who could scarcely be forty ...

'I was admiring your painting of Hector Pleys—just the other day. It's super.'

He looked pleased. 'Why, thank you. A piece of luck, that one, just because he knew the family. An obligement, really, since I *was* young then. Heavens, I can see a million faults in it now.' He shuddered delicately. 'Ah well, that's the way it goes with prodigies. They have a compensating obscurity in middle age and usually die unknown. Perhaps they reach the peak of fame before their powers of tenacity are properly developed—believe me, once at the top you need a certain ruthlessness to stay there. It's one of the ironies in life,' he added sadly, 'that prodigies, in common with old soldiers, rarely die, they only fade away.' He smiled, shook himself like a dog shaking off fear and asked: 'How are you going to enjoy working for Marie?'

I said: 'Oh, she's a dear and Priory House is absolutely super.'

He looked pleased. 'But rather isolated for a girl of your age.'

I protested that I like solitude, anyway only children were used to it. As he listened, he took my arm and led the way towards the sandy track leading to Priory House. On our right the sea glittered, metallic, grey as pewter. Holy Island seemed far away, sleepy, retreating into the dreams of an early night.

'Watch your stockings.' As he led the way he turned, his smile slow but brilliant, showing excellent teeth in that sombre Borderer's face, where laughter looked like a new invention. I realised he was older than I had thought at first glance. Forty perhaps. Older—and more vulnerable. Smaller too, a mere six feet tall, as if a Dracula creature of the night must need a horse and falcon to give him strength, and a swirling deadly mist to bring the illusion of mystery, the power of a legend come to life.

Unrepentant, I saw that I had been guilty again, up to my old tricks of building an ordinary man into fantasy hero. Still, every pleased smile from him brought that faint twitch from the region of my heart and I realised, even in the late afternoon of a space-age world, that where the Adam Hebburns of the human race were concerned, be it twelfth or twentieth century, the villagers at Whitton Sands and points adjacent probably locked up their daughters at night. I found my lips curving at the idea and blushed when his look was suddenly intense.

'Sorry to keep staring,' he said, 'the shadowy light plays tricks. You look like someone I know ...'

I dragged off the white headscarf and he gave a little sigh. Of relief, I thought later. 'We have met before,' and when he frowned I added: 'Don't you remember? A few weeks ago? One misty evening on the road to Whitton Peel I got lost. My car, a red Mini, was in the ditch and you helped me. I don't know what I would have done if you hadn't come along. And then there were other ...' I stopped, embarrassed, knowing as I saw him clearly again that this was the same man who had driven a white car through the streets of Corham several times. Slowly, looking for someone ...

'Of course,' he mumbled absently without looking at me. 'That must be it.'

There was an awkward silence and I asked shyly: 'How did you know where to find me?'

'Where to find you?' he asked sharply. 'What do you mean—where?'

'Up at the Priory.'

'Oh—yes, I see,' he stumbled. His laugh wasn't quite steady either. 'Of course. Marie sent me after you.' He gave me a hard look. 'What was the matter back there? What frightened you?'

'I thought for a moment you were the Crusader's ghost. I'm not joking—you ought to warn visitors he's the image of you.'

He jerked a thumb towards the great arch behind us. 'You mean old Adam de Hebbyrne? My very remote ancestor?'

When he laughed I said, 'I know it sounds foolish, but that night when I was lost I'd been to the Peel Tower for help and the Hermit

105

wouldn't answer the door. I was scared and took to my heels, then in all that mist I started remembering Ninespears Crag and the legend of King Arthur. I expect I was in the right mood for the grues and when you rode straight at me ...'

He chuckled. 'No wonder you were scared. You thought I was old Arthur with my knights hell-bent on saving England ...'

'One hardly expects horses and falcons on nicely tarmacked modern roads. It isn't a bit nice on a witches' brew of a night.'

'But even modern horses need exercising,' he said. 'The weather had been abominable and poor Starlight hates the rain. She'd been restless all day. It was thundery, close ...'

'It must have been. You weren't even wearing a jacket.'

He laughed. 'Exercising a horse around Ninespears Crag is no gentle canter, lady. There are bogs and ditches and gates to negotiate. It's hot work. It's a wonder you didn't go rushing off for the police or the Psychical Research Society.' He grinned. 'What did your folks say about *that* encounter?'

'I didn't tell them. They're very sensible and would have thought their little girl was suffering from hallucinations—or an overdose of gin.'

'Well, I've been called many things in my time, I suppose "hallucination" is more flattering than some. So you really think I'm like the Crusader?'

'You're a little more animated, thank goodness. But take a misty night, a horse and Hereward screaming blue murder on your wrist ...'

His eyebrows raised. 'Fancy you remember Hereward's name. He will be pleased. Poor old Hereward, he's been in a bad way lately. Got himself chased by a pair of golden eagles who nest on the Crag. He's a snoopy bird and never learns to mind his own business—anyway, for once he lost his head and plummeted down straight through some trees. It's a wonder he didn't break his silly neck, but he landed safely on a tricky bit of marsh up near the Crag. Nothing worse than a mashed-up tail, his flight feathers broken. I'd never have found him except that the predatory birds, hoodie crows and the like were considering him as supper. Took half an hour to get to him, one false move and you're sunk in bog to the ears. I only hoped one of the eagles patiently circling the air wouldn't get up an appetite and beat me to him ...'

'Eagles, I didn't know there were any here.'

107

'Hush, the wildlife people don't like it generally known. We've had this pair for years. They used to be tame, the owner bred them in captivity and let them out for film work, but now they're wild and free. They're good at keeping to themselves but get mad at peregrines poaching on their preserves. Times are hard for eagles, too.'

'Peregrines?'

'Yes, falcon is the female bird, so don't insult old Hereward, will you? He's very sensitive about his masculinity. Actually the peregrine is rather smaller than the female'—he grinned—'and as with some other species, including the human, not so deadly.'

'You must be joking,' I said unprovoked. 'Will Hereward fly again?'

'Oh, sure, the stupid clot. I have a falconer friend in Berwick who has given him an artificial tail good as new. It's rather like having teeth crowned, the new feathers are "imped" into the quills of the old tail.'

I remembered the parrot perch in the studio. I really hadn't used my wits very much. He had stopped talking and was staring at me again in that hard brooding way. 'Am I very like her?' I asked. When he looked embarrassed I said cheerfully, as if I had forgotten his hands

108

around my throat, his words 'I thought I was rid of you for ever', at our first encounter: 'Diane made the same mistake from the distance. She met me on the Brandy Road and thought I was Melanie.'

His face darkened. 'How did you know it was called the Brandy Road?' he asked sharply.

'Strachan, at the Whitton Arms, told me.'

'Oh.' A pause. 'Did Diane tell you about Melanie?' His voice was still sharp and just a little cross. When I said no, he laughed. Was there relief in it, was he considerably pleased that I wasn't Melanie?

'Diane is chronically short-sighted but too vain to wear her glasses out of doors.' He looked at me again. 'Still, it's a remarkable coincidence.' And the next moment I was forgotten, he was walking quickly, biting his lip. Absorbed in some private vision. Of hell and Melanie, I thought, as he forgot to adapt his long easy stride to my shorter step and I was left behind with some new uneasy thoughts. Something had changed in the last few moments, turning us into strangers, no longer friendly, at ease with each other. What? Odd that three people had been deeply shocked by my likeness to Melanie. Diane, Marie and Philip Riche. But Adam most of all. Where did it all fit—would I ever find out in my brief stay why I had brought such panic to Priory House?

As we approached the garden, Whitton Peel was visible through the trees. Despite the reassurance, spiky evidence of the twentieth century in television masts and telephone wires, it looked lifeless and abandoned.

'How's the old man?'

'What old man?' asked Adam, his mind elsewhere.

'Your inhospitable hermit who terrified the life out of me.'

'Oh, Jim Elliott, you mean. I imagine he's fine.'

'Is he very old?'

Adam thought. 'No-o. Elderly, one might say.'

'What brought it about?'

'What brought *what* about?' he asked cautiously.

'The recluse thing. Was it a sad love affair or some base black deed in his terrible past?'

'You read too many novels, don't you.' And his voice cold but amused, dismissed my questions as prying and ill-bred.

We were silent for a few steps, then in defence of romance I said: 'I wasn't prying, I'm just sorry for him. It's awfully sad to be old and alone.'

'It can be sad to be young and alone too. Don't worry about our hermit. People look after him very well. They really do care, that's one of the advantages of village life. There's always someone.'

'You weren't born here though, were you? You're an American.'

'Well, well. So a sharp ear goes with that eagle eye. No wonder Hereward was charmed by you. Yes, ma'am, despite the Crusader and the imposing family background, I was born in California,' he said nasally, putting it on. 'I'd never set eyes on my native heath until I was grown.'

'You've lost most of your accent, too.'

'Fifteen years in the wilds of Northumberland, ma'am.' He laughed and added, 'You make it sound like something I should be glad to be rid of. Not that I ever had much accent. Both my parents are from this area. Grandpa still going strong in Berwick.'

'Where are your parents now?'

'Back in La Jolla. My father's an engineer, nothing romantic about him.'

He opened the gate for me and I asked: 'Haven't I seen you recently? Driving through Corham?'

'I shouldn't think so. Corham,' he repeated innocently, as if after fifteen years he had never heard of its famous Abbey, in better preservation than the ancient monument behind us, and the old Roman settlement by the river. 'Corham. Is that where you're from?'

'Yes.' How odd that Marie hadn't told him. 'I thought I recognised you a couple of times ...' And I wasn't to be put off this time by an evasive shrug. 'A white car, a Kharmann Ghia,' I insisted, 'driving along the main street.'

He smiled at that, a slow winning smile. 'A female with a remarkable eye for cars, I see. Most of you say vaguely a big white car or a little white car, with a Mini or VW the ultimate in recognition. Even Melanie, with her passion for speed, couldn't be specific about identifying them. She said car brands bored her.'

I didn't pursue the subject of his visits to Corham, instead I asked the predictable question, feeling entitled to an answer, having been so readily mistaken for her.

'Didn't Marie tell you?' He paused and looked up at the sky with narrowed eyes, as if searching for something among the gathering storm clouds. 'Melanie is my wife. One of her friends had a small plane, a Chipmunk. It crashed last month,' he jerked a thumb

112

seawards, 'over there. She intended going with Bob Myers that day, but only his body has been recovered.' I vaguely remembered having read something about a missing plane in the local papers.

'I'm sorry,' I said. And as he gnawed his lip in the ensuing silence, I wondered if this indicated that he was absorbed by a thought not new to him. If Melanie wasn't in the plane, then where was she?

'I'm sorry,' I repeated for something to say.

In acknowledgment, his lips extended a fraction on either side of his mouth—the quickest neatest smile of complete dismissal I had ever seen. 'I hope you're good at spelling, Marie is hopeless. I'm doing the illustrations for her book and we'll probably commit some shocking *faux pas* if someone doesn't keep us right. I hear you're exemplary ...'

We had reached the pretty garden with its nest of leaves overlooked by the study window. So Melanie was his wife, the garden seat, painted white and curiously forlorn, seemed the very texture of waiting. And for me it all clicked neatly into place ...

Melanie was his wife and sometime model. A red-headed girl, with great green slanting eyes, framed by autumn leaves, beautiful, haunting, rather sad. A famous picture and one I had seen often, reproduced in colour magazine supplements or in art shops' windows in Newcastle. Now I remembered the title that my parents had forgotten:

'The October Witch.'

I looked at Adam, imagining their lives together, the beautiful model and temperamental demanding artist. I didn't much fancy Melanie's score in an encounter with her masterful husband. I knew from experience that in a rage he could be cold and deadly. All this polite sweetness and light had its darker moments. I would remember for ever his hands at my throat, his words: 'What sepulchre in hell opened and let you loose ...'

I wondered what Warren, sternly coping with traffic demeanours and the poachers who were Corham's contribution to crime, would make of that statement. What would he say now to his jeering dismissal of my Horseman as 'imagination'. 'Sure you didn't take the wrong turning and meet a miner on a bike, carrying a canary?' Indeed!

I had a nasty feeling there was a place for me in the weird human jigsaw being played out in Priory House, for as we turned the corner I realised someone was lying.

114

Outside the front door, brazenly white and shining, was a sight that made all the blood in my body run ice-cold, right down to the soles of my feet.

The car was a Kharmann Ghia, and, what is more, I have an excellent memory for registration numbers too.

'Why, that's the car I saw you driving,' I said.

He frowned hard at it for a moment, then at me. Faintly bored now, with all that friendly sparkle faded, like a house with the shutters pulled down. He had done the polite thing, got me safely back to Priory House at his sister's request.

'Really,' he said with a shrug, 'I expect Corham's so small I drove through the main street without even noticing it. Quite a coincidence,' he added in a matter-of-fact tone.

Somewhere deep inside me I felt anger rise. My likeness to Melanie and his likeness to the Crusader might well be dismissed as coincidence, but he was pretty free with his other 'coincidences'.

Life just isn't so obliging. Some human hand with a quick clever human mind behind it had contrived my appearance at Whitton Sands. I followed him into the house, uncomfortably aware that for some sinister purpose or purposes unknown to me, *I was bait.*

CHAPTER 6

Melanie was a ghost with my face no longer. Pieced together from fragments of conversation and impressions I was building up an image of a highly strung elemental woman. The exotic clothes and perfume, 'The October Witch', all suggested a frail but passionate woman, her beauty the perfect foil for Adam's strength and the ruthlessness his face suggested. I imagined quick flaring tempers, resulting in indescribable scenes.

Even the manner of her death was in keeping with her personality, dramatic, extravagant, and utterly wasteful. Impossible that one so vividly alive should leave the world without trace. And I thought sadly of Shakespeare's: 'Golden lads and lasses must like chimney sweepers come to dust ...'

As I followed Adam into the kitchen, Marie was deftly moving her wheelchair, directing operations for Diane, who was draining potatoes at the sink. She emerged from clouds of steam and hurled herself at Adam with the unrestrained exuberance of a small child.

'Uncle Adam, you're exactly on time.' Then, over his shoulder, she saw me and remarked in tones of bleak disappointment: 'Oh, I see you've met Miss Marsden.' Since Marie must have told her Adam had gone in search of me, I could only assume she had hoped I had got permanently lost between the house and the ruined Priory. Even my praise of her share in the subsequent meal did nothing to destroy the misery on her face. Every time she looks at me, I thought, she hates me because I'm not Melanie.

As we ate there was some desultory talk about Hereward's new tail and the farming grandfather's health, which I gathered was the reason for Adam's hasty overnight visit to Berwick. I also learned something of the heredity which breeds men like Adam Hebburn.

'The old man will be ninety in December,' he said. 'They don't make them like that any more. He still runs that farm practically single-handed and is up at dawn every day ...' He talked with more authority, and more wistfulness, than I would have expected about farming matters and Diane capped the conversation with—what I considered for a parson's daugh-

118

ter—a rather risque story about mating cows.

Adam laughed, asked for a second helping of lemon meringue pie, and Diane leaped to her feet with a look of pure adoration. She carried on a gay bantering, and rather flirtatious, conversation with him. She certainly wasn't in awe of the great Adam Hebburn and when she disappeared into the kitchen to make coffee Marie smiled as if apology was due to me for her exuberance.

'Her father visits his parishioners most afternoons. Outlying farms, sick people, you know. So Diane makes the meal when she comes home from school, it's excellent practice for her and, of course, she adores being here. The members of her father's little flock,' she added with a completely serious face, 'are rather lavish with their hospitality ...'

'By which you mean whisky,' said Adam, tilting an amused eyebrow in her direction.

'Really, Adam, what a thing to say.' Her tone Best Outraged Victoriana.

'Nonsense, dear. I'm sure Julie won't fly in terror from a parson who drinks. It's just one of our less well-kept secrets and she's liable to smell it when they meet. She has sharp eyes and ears,' he said, considering me, 'and doubtless a sharp nose to match. Anyway, it's

119

nothing new for a parson to like his liquor. Until times modern in these parts it was considered the best qualification for the job. The respectable parson was usually the smugglers' best friend and undoubtedly their best customer.'

I thought of Philip Riche whispering: 'Watch the wall, my darling, as the gentlemen go by.' Wasn't it from a poem about: 'Brandy for the parson ...?'

'Mr. Scales is a very fine man,' said Marie, eyeing her brother sternly. 'A very fine man.'

'And who's denying it? Drunk or sober, he's no hypocrite. Why all the mad pretence that parsons aren't like the rest of men and entitled to their share of human weaknesses?' Adam paused to help himself to more wine. 'After all, Marie, I drink too,' he held up his glass and surveyed the contents narrowly, 'and I think I'm a very fine man.'

Marie laughed and leaning over patted his hand. 'So you are, brother dear. So you are.'

As they exchanged affectionate glances, I wondered could I possibly have misheard her sombre conversation with Philip Riche, how they could never be happy together: 'While he is still alive'? Marie Hebburn must be a supreme actress, I thought bitterly, to behave in this manner and yet secretly wish her brother dead.

In the kitchen after Diane's departure I stacked willow-pattern plates on the oak dresser, wondering morbidly what would be her reception at the vicarage. How does a drunken parson behave? Would he be maudlin and sentimental, or madly biblical, spewing up great thundering texts and prophecies?

As I tidied the ancient tranquil kitchen, with its stone floor and its hooks in beams for bygone gastronomical pleasures of whole carcasses and hams, I was pleased that the Hebburns had not committed the folly of savage modernisation. Plastics existed, utilitarian but discreet, while copper, chintz and the old-fashioned 'rag' mats, common to thousands of working-class Northern kitchens, were prominently, lovingly, in evidence.

One would have expected more opulence generally, but perhaps good taste and not lack of money had decided the Hebburns to keep within the ancient spirit of the house. Against all odds, it seemed a happy place, and as I went through to the lounge I was conscious again of its tranquil atmosphere, certain from my earliest days that houses, like people, have souls which must not be offended. There was certainly nothing remaining of the disquiet which must have marked its smuggling days. In the ancient oak-panelled lounge, late roses nodded sleepily in a copper bowl at the still open window, making the empty room a suitable place to linger and dream.

But not for long. The door behind me opened unceremoniously.

'Ah, the new lassie, is it?' I turned to see Strachan, who came between me and my peacefully nodding roses. At his heavy step one of the petals, red as blood, fell on to the table. I had a sudden sense of outrage as he snatched it contemptuously and crushed it between his large fingers.

'The new lassie,' he repeated, looking me over. 'And how are ye, hinny? Enjoyin' yersel'?' The close-set button-black eyes danced with amusement at my discomfort. 'Fine house, this. I hear you're not here for ornament either, that ye do a bit o' typing.' He stepped back and bellowed noisily, his whole body shaking as if he found the idea excruciatingly funny. 'Mebbe you'll come and do some letters for me, just when Adam can spare ye, like,' he added, wagging a finger at me, his leering face inches away from my own.

I was aware of a dark shadow behind us. 'Well, Strachan, and what can we do for you?

I didn't hear you knock at the door when you came in.' The words were polite enough, but not even Strachan could have thought Adam's chilly face savoured of welcome.

I excused myself hastily, but neither of them seemed to notice my departure. As I closed the door, Strachan's voice raised in anger said: 'I know I'm not acceptable—damned high-and-mightiness—despite our close relationship,' and to Adam's protesting mutter, added: 'Damn it, we don't want the whole of Whitton Sands to know. Don't think a man of my age would climb all the blasted way up the Brandy Road either, if there was any other way.'

Footsteps, so I hastily retreated to the kitchen and closed the door. I looked around, seeking the reassurance its comfort and serenity had brought earlier, but now the atmosphere had changed. I knew why. I was frightened by something more than Strachan's unpleasant manner. A disquieting small voice inside whispered: There's something mysterious going on here. These Hebburns are an odd lot, and no mistake, despite their fine manners. I thought I had hit on the answer and felt P.C. Warren Browne and my amateur detective father would both be very proud of my intuition that smuggling was somehow involved. I could hear Mum's warning voice plainly across forty miles: 'Your curiosity will get you into trouble one of these days, Julie.' And 'by the pricking of my thumbs', for 'trouble' I was inclined to substitute a stronger word: danger.

Small wonder I dreamed of Melanie. Her bedroom was certainly haunted. It never rested as bedrooms should. The window seemed to catch every breeze within miles and swirled the leaves like ghostly steps in the little garden below. And always the echoing boom of sea, the sad eternal torment of wave upon rock, wave upon rock ...

Lying snug but wakefully conscious in the comfortable bed, over a final cigarette I remembered the strange adventures of the day. In particular that my ghostly horseman should be Adam Hebburn of all people. And not an elderly artist, but an attractive man of forty, possibly a widower, who liked me too. In such circumstances, even the dream of a decently far-off happy ending seemed permissible. With Melanie dead, I wasn't coveting my neighbour's husband either. It was all so neat and easy. Too easy.

Presumably the vividness of the dream belonged to the moment before sleep when I thought drowsily of poor Melanie and all her

124

exotic, luxurious possessions waiting sad and forlorn for her return. Wouldn't it be awful if one of those wardrobe doors burst open and she sprang out demanding like one of Goldilock's Three Bears: 'Who's been Sleeping in My Bed?'

Then came the dream. So sickeningly real that for days afterwards I could hardly face those closed doors in the bedroom without horror. As I slept they slowly opened and Melanie stepped out. She came over to the bed, menacing, a kind of zombie, open-eyed but dead. I stretched out my hands to thrust her away and as I touched her she crumbled. Where she had stood a pile of fine white sand and a heap of empty clothes, glittering, still moving with the expensive stir of rich material, the air heavy with perfume. I remember looking at them, grateful even in my horror that there was nobody to dispose of. Until I noticed ten small white twigs spread out like fingers on the carpet, the skeletal bones of her hands as she fell ...

I slept little after that and put in an early appearance downstairs, hoping to impress my employers, neither of whom was visible. Mrs. Miles was already at work in the kitchen. She had grey cropped hair and her eyes were an

125

exact match. Her hair so definite a colour that one is in continual doubt whether even in child- and girl-hood it could ever have been any other than grey. She was solidly built and her apple cheeks testified to a well-spent healthy country life. Her conversation hinted at education and sophistication, too, and Marie told me later she had been wardrobe mistress with a Shake-spearean company. She certainly did not con-sider herself a 'daily woman', but referred to Mr. Adam and Miss Marie 'and my other ladies' as being 'looked after' by her. She in-cluded in this list 'the parson and that poor child Diane', as if it were a Christian duty and nothing so sordid as hard cash changed hands in payment for her labours.

'I hope you'll be happy here. Just a week or two, isn't it? Winters can be very isolated and lonely for a young person.' She eyed me solemn but friendly. 'They didn't tell me until yesterday. Never a word,' she added reproach-fully. 'If I had known I would have prepared the bedroom for you. Miss Marie has never mentioned to me that she needed a secretary. An older lady would be better in this lonely place,' she added with another doubtful look, as if I had sinned already in her eyes by being young.

126

She picked up a shabby cap. 'Ah, I see Strachan was here.' I hoped she wasn't going to ask me to return it, but she hung it behind the door and said: 'It can wait, he'll get it when he comes to lunch tomorrow.'

If she had announced that a dinosaur would sit down to lunch with us, I couldn't have been more surprised. Suddenly she smiled: 'I see you've met. You'd better get used to Strachan, he's a rough-looking customer, but in a manner of speaking he's a member of the family. Most folks look surprised when they hear he's Mr. Adam's father-in-law, Melanie's dad.'

Incredible that such a gross uncouth character as Strachan could have sired Melanie's delicate gossamer beauty, and, as if reading my mind, Mrs. Miles laughed: 'Actually he's her step-father. They used to live in this house when Melanie was a child, when it was still the inn. Although it's been in the Hebburn family for generations, this house is only two hundred years old, built on the foundations of Whitton Castle. The Peel Tower is all that's left of the original Castle and my late husband, who was keen on local history, used to tell me that underneath here,' she tapped her foot on the floor, 'underneath here is riddled with passages and rooms, the dungeons of the old Castle,

127

some of them leading right down to the sea. The smugglers knew the way through the caves, but it's lost now. Mr. Adam's great-grandfather was a bit of a puritan, not like the earlier Hebburns, who helped the smugglers.

'Yes, they often forgot which side they were on and whether they owed allegiance to the English or the Scots king, sometimes brother fought against brother. A Hebburn fought for the Old Pretender and died trying to get the Stuarts back on to the English throne. Those were bad days for a lot of Northumbrian gentlemen.' She gave me a bright smile. 'I suppose people had just as many troubles and sorrows then as they do now. Take poor Miss Marie, always sweet and smiling, with such a cheerful heart after all her suffering ...'

The door opened and Diane bounced in to deposit a large carton of groceries on the table. 'So you've met Miss Marsden. Does she remind you of anyone?' she asked, as if I weren't present.

Mrs. Miles looked at me. 'Wait until I get my glasses. There now,' she settled them firmly and stared for a moment. 'Is it a film star, Miss Diane? No? That's fine, because I'm not much for the pictures these days.' She sighed. 'I used to know all the great stars once.

Stage and screen.'

'Look again,' said Diane impatiently. 'Isn't she like Melanie?'

Mrs. Miles considered, shook her head. 'No. Her hair is dark and Melanie's red as a carrot, with green eyes too. She's not a bit like her.'

Diane looked rather angry, as if there was something personal in this refusal to see my resemblance, while Mrs. Miles stared at me somehow fascinated. 'I've only once seen eyes the exact colour of yours,' she whispered dreamily.

From outside, the pip-pip of an impatient car. 'My transport,' said Diane, 'I must rush.'

'You were saying?' I asked Mrs. Miles. She jerked into reality. 'No, no—nothing really. I can't remember ...' and was obviously relieved but somehow scared when Marie wheeled herself in, looking for Adam, and bustled to the sink, ignoring us both.

'I haven't anything ready for you, Julie,' said Marie. 'See if Adam wants any letters typed. Can you remember the way to the studio?'

Adam wasn't there but Hereward greeted me like an old friend, bounding back and forth on his perch delightedly: 'Kek, kek—kek, kek,' he chattered when I stroked his head and admired his new tail. 'Kek, kek, *kek.*' Pleased and excited by an admirer, he ruffled his feathers and rolled a coy bright eye at me.

Again I was struck by the neat soullessness of the room, boards and easel stacked away against the walls. On a shelf some large books gathering dust. I opened one with a strange sense of excitement. The yellowing pages contained pencil drawings of a girl. Profile, hands, hair—little rough sketches, the kind a competent artist can produce in a couple of minutes, yet catch the spirit of the sitter completely. There she was, legs tucked under her, sitting at a table reading, although the hair fell over her face, it was recognisably the same girl and the book pleased her, for her expression was smiling. In another she lay on her stomach on the floor, ankles crossed with an oddly childlike pose of preoccupation.

I skipped some pages, and she looked at me from the bedroom window, staring down into the garden. Anxious, twisting a strand of long hair through her fingers ... There were many more, a series of small masterpieces, lovingly, expertly drawn. The date, fifteen years ago.

The girl was undoutedly Melanie. In another book, notes regarding colours and drawings of leaves, the notes Adam had used for 'The October Witch'. It was strange, but I could almost feel the idea taking shape, slowly at first, then reaching a crescendo of creation. Sadly, I noticed how obsessed he had been with her. He didn't seem inclined to draw anyone or anything else. How he must have loved her ...

The last book I opened was three years old, long after her painting's rise and fall from fame. But Adam still drew her, desperately now. Wild, erratic drawings, searching for a gimmick, for something new to say, some hardly recognisable as Melanie, some impatiently, savagely scored out. Quickly I laid it aside. It was like looking into a tortured soul. As if Adam Hebburn was still conjuring up his October Witch, or, worse, trying to exorcise her.

'So this is where you are.' It was Adam.

'I'm just admiring the view. It's such a perfect room for an artist,' I said hastily, conscious of my undeniable snooping.

'Do you paint at all?' he asked, and I told him I was hopeless. He looked disappointed and said no, he hadn't any letters for me but perhaps Mrs. Miles could use some help—if I didn't mind working in the kitchen.

As we prepared lunch, there was the noisy drone of a plane overhead, flying low, and Mrs. Miles paused mid-sentence and wiping floury hands on her apron rushed to the back door and stood watching the sky.

'Just another of those training planes from the airport. They all sound the same as Bob's.' She closed the door. 'Funny, you know I always expect her to be up there. Flying too low, taking risks. I just can't believe she's gone.'

'It must have been terrible for you all. Such a tragedy.'

She looked at me sadly. 'Well, we had got used to Miss Melanie's little ways. She never did anything according to plan. Even as a small girl she liked to frighten folk by doing the unexpected. A practical joker if ever was—and sometimes not all that kind, either. You expect children to grow out of such daftness, but she never did. Even as a grown-up, as a sensible married woman who should know better, she liked her bit of mischief, or to worry folk. She loved that.' Her nice homely face was suddenly sharp and angry. 'Yes, it would be just like her to come back, when everyone is getting on fine.' She sighed. 'It's not very nice and all rather morbid, but until her body is recovered, she's only presumed dead. Only poor Mr. Myers, the pilot, and bits and pieces of the plane have drifted ashore ...'

She broke off as Adam looked in through the window and waved to us, on his way through the garden. I felt slightly weak about the knees. I was far too susceptible to this man.

What if Melanie wasn't dead? I could hear her mocking laughter as she watched me slyly, heartlessly, packing my suitcase. Knowing that I loved Adam and that her most superb practical joke had found the perfect victim. And Adam, quite unaware, indifferent to my misery, would be watching her with adoring eyes, marvelling at her miraculous return ...

At my side, Mrs. Miles whispered: 'Isn't it awful to think she's still out there somewhere?'

'Yes.' I shivered. 'Awful.'

And that was the moment I got it clearly into my head that Melanie was certainly 'out there somewhere'. Waiting to come back. Waiting her chance.

Very much alive ...

CHAPTER 7

Marie wrote and Adam drew, his wild flowers curiously bloodless, as if he had used up all his exotic passions in 'The October Witch'. Meanwhile, I typed notes, prepared an index, made a bibliography and checked botanial names. Adam had been right about one thing. Their spelling was atrocious.

And so every day that passed saw me an integrated part of the Hebburn household, on the surface a normal busy family undramatically adhering to a well-established routine. There was little personal incident except frequent telephone calls to and from my parents. And from Warren, suspiciously demanding how much longer I intended staying away. His tone of constant reproof implied wilful spite on my part and a deliberate attempt to avoid him.

Several times I had to deter him from a 'run out on the motor-bike' in his off-duty hours. I didn't want him in Priory House, spoiling my magic, perhaps making me see Adam Hebburn as less than heroic. Warren was very persistent about coming on Sunday. I mentioned this to Marie, who looked at my doleful face and said:

'Oh, what a pity. Adam is planning something special for us, I think,' she added mysteriously, with that brilliant sweet smile which stressed a usually unremarkable resemblance to her brother.

'Sorry. Too busy,' I duly informed Warren, then I washed my hair and considered suitable clothes for Adam's 'treat'. But Sunday came and went as just another working day, its only drama a sudden gale that lashed the sea into a ferment of great frothy waves and stripped the little garden of its last shreds of colour. The bright leaves were all gone, only muted browns of stubble field and sour moor remained, bordered by great black cobwebbed intricacies of hedgerow and tree. Over an almost colourless sky, like something from a faded water-colour, the seagulls' noisy chuckles echoed, vanishing in the direction of the Farne Islands. Holy Island dominated the sea no longer but shrouded itself into the mists of autumn, suggesting a once-elegant woman glad that the harsh light of summer no longer showed up her threadbare wardrobe.

If behind-the-scenes dramas existed in Priory

House they never obtruded. Even Philip Riche's visits to Marie, whenever Adam was absent in Berwick, became a commonplace intrigue. Such circumstances coloured those early intuitions as my usual over-strong imagination and, walking down the Brandy Road to shop in the village or post letters, the only remaining mystery was why Melanie's body had not been washed up by the tide, far on the beach below.

Whenever I looked at the sea I pictured that tiny plane hurtling down, disappearing into a great spume of foam, and then the silence, the ripple of waves. Then nothing. I thought of the horror of rushing down through the sky, being trapped and knowing that certain death was inevitable as the sea came nearer, nearer. I wondered morbidly if Melanie fought and screamed, or if she laughed in the face of oblivion, believing herself to be immortal.

Then one day, with all my senses lulled, I had an adventure with a Peeping Tom. Often I sat at the bedroom windows that had been Melanie's, fascinated by the view. Eastwards, the untidy ragged garden below and, beyond it, the sea. And northwards, Ninespears Crag in autumn melancholy, with its dots of white sheep and emerald patches of marshland. In the foreground, taking a bird's-eye view of us now that the intervening trees were bare, was Whitton Peel.

One of the windows seemed to look directly into my bedroom, as if keeping it under close scrutiny. When one has spent most of a lifetime with neighbours it is an instinctive action to draw bedroom curtains at night and even by day. I found the lack of privacy disturbing. However, presumably for admiration of an uninterrupted view, neither curtain rail nor pelmet existed, nor any evidence that either window had ever been covered. Suddenly I felt as if eyes watched me, the tempting window-seats so thoughtfully provided seeming too close for comfort to that dark tower across the way. That somehow *attentive* tower, secret, leaning ...

Occasionally its shadowy garden had an occupant, a figure shrouded in a grey hooded cassock. On a dull sunless day, bent and shambling, he looked less than human and stronger nerves than mine might have toyed with the possibility of Whitton Peel being haunted, taking little comfort from the supposition that ghosts don't walk at midday. Then I noticed the hooded shape at the window, motionless and apparently staring straight across

137

into my bedroom. I fled downstairs and on each occasion when I returned the window at Whitton Peel was empty. At the beginning I told myself I was being fanciful, perhaps the light was catching a robe hanging in direct line with the window. After all, humans don't stay motionless for considerable periods. Unless they are on the look-out for something—or someone.

Eventually I concluded it couldn't be anyone else but the Hermit and decided to ask Marie for some screens for the window.

'They would have to be specially made. Melanie loathed curtains, said it ruined a marvellous view,' she added apologetically.

'It also ruins a marvellous chance for a *voyeur.*'

Marie frowned. 'I don't understand.' And when I told her that the Hermit stared into my room for hours on end, and I suspected used field glasses for a better look, she said: 'How annoying, I'll mention it to Adam.' But she seemed neither annoyed nor particularly surprised.

Later Adam said: 'You must be mistaken, Julie. Why should anyone in Whitton Peel want to do that?'

'You're a man, Adam. Perhaps you know the answer to why men abandon the world, for what strange inexplicable reasons—apart from a stricken love affair, which is the romantic answer most women would provide ...'

'Nonsense. That weird attire is probably only a dressing-gown. After all, it's damned cold here in winter.'

'Well, perhaps it isn't too hard to stay holed up in Whitton Peel with fresh milk and newspapers every day. A radio, telephone and the telly. It might well be cold in winter, but I think your hermit is far from the poor old man in a cave beloved of legends. He's managed very nicely to extract the best of both worlds.'

Adam murmured, 'Sharp eyes again.' And as I expounded on my theory I saw his face. He looked bored and tired, no—not tired, defeated. For no reason I understood, I was sorry for him, sorry I had started this talk that bored him. Hastily, to reinstate myself, I said: 'What a fuss, I expect he's only a thwarted Peeping Tom.'

'Only a sick, sick person would do that sort of thing and I can assure you our hermit means no harm to anyone.' He looked sharply towards the tower. 'Anyway, it won't happen again. You have my assurance.'

And although I saw the grey figure in the garden, there was no more window-watching.

But my curiosity about Adam Hebburn was aroused even more. As a child I always wanted to know what made the clock tick, and, as I grew older, clocks were replaced by people. Even if I hadn't been head over heels in love with Adam I would still have been intrigued by the enigma of a man who could control the vagaries of mysterious hermits but hadn't much success nearer home, with someone like Melanie.

He invited me along to watch Hereward being flown and as we walked along the cliffs, I looked at that rugged profile—an improbable artist, the face suggested a fighting Borderer, a soldier or a pirate born out of his time, confined by some trick of fate into the inaction and curious obscurity of the present.

Perhaps I could have dismissed the episode with the Hermit, the dramas I suspected, that Marie and Philip both wished Adam dead and Adam's own hatred of his missing wife, as exaggerations of my taste for melodrama. But there was one thing I could not dismiss, a haunting inexplicable fear that my arrival in Whitton Sands had been far from coincidental and, as time passed, so did intuition mount that I had been brought here for some purpose, *because of my likeness to Melanie.*

But how had Adam known precisely where to lay hands on a girl like her? Judging by his initial rough handling of me, it seemed unlikely that it was a mere attraction for the same type. Then it dawned that as I worked in a bookshop in the main street of Corham, the nearest town within forty miles to Whitton Sands—and, despite his denial, Adam could have seen me there any time as he drove through—perhaps he had already marked me down *before Melanie vanished.* After all, only one body had been recovered and as Bob Myers had a private air-field, nobody saw them take off together, and there was only Melanie's statement that she *intended* going with him on a flight. I would have given much to know whom she had originally told, whether it was one person or several. Or whether it was Adam alone ...

Yet surely I would have remembered Adam, however long ago we had met, however accidentally. Dear God, he wasn't the kind of man any woman between seventeen and seventy could overlook. If he had been a customer in the shop I would certainly have noticed him over-large in those narrow alleys of shelves. No, to have tracked me down to Marsden's Bookshop needed more explanation than this easy one.

Then with a feeling of sheer triumph I had the answer. I remembered his painting of the dead actor Hector Pleys. And, of course, it all fitted after that. He knew the family, he had told me himself, and that was why he was commissioned to paint the portrait.

From Hector it was one step to his sister. Lady Ester Pleys. I recalled our last meeting, her nervous flurry of questions whether I could work for her writer friend. So Lady Ester had been asked to negotiate my employment. But if that were correct then my intuition was quite, quite wrong and my presence at Priory House was innocent, my resemblance to Melanie mere coincidence, even if it had frightened the life out of so many people. There wasn't any question of chicanery if the Pleys were involved ... I wondered for a moment if the Hebburns had 'something on her', were using blackmail to make her exert her influence on Julie Marsden for some shady purpose. I chuckled out loud, even my imagination boggled at Lady Ester as Queen of the Smugglers.

At my side, Adam withdrew his troubled gaze from the sea. 'So you're amused. Out with it. I could use a joke and you haven't uttered since we left the house.'

'I was just thinking Hereward has a distinctly

human expression. Don't you think so?' I said hastily. He said no and I prattled on: 'Hasn't autumn a simply marvellous smell?' He laughed and the mellow sun cast over the blighted heath a delightful orange glow which made Adam in his sheepskin jacket look flatteringly young.

We were on the edge of the moor. Below us the Brandy Road dipped sharply down to the sea over a white cliffside, sliced off and pitted with caves like some giant Gruyère cheese. I looked back at the house. 'It all looks exactly as it did my first day here. Beautiful, but no longer breath-taking ... How sad, I seem to have grown used to it, even in a short time.'

'You make it sound like a long dull marriage,' he said, his face sombre again, so that I wondered where the margin for error in a marriage ended, what sort of cruelties and humiliations turned love into indifference or, worse, into hatred. He saw my shocked expression and laughing softly took my arm. 'That's not a pretty frown, Julie girl. You're looking like someone else who doesn't expect the magic of first illusions to last very long.' He paused. 'So I was right. Even at your age it's as well to know that first impressions can be wrong, but if we're lucky by the time we find out something permanent and worth while has taken their place. Artists know more about illusions than most people, to their cost. You toy with a dream that only just eludes you, sure you've got the answer to it all in something wonderful, a world-shaking idea. Then next morning you look for it, but bang, it's stone dead. People are like that too, some of them—not many, thank God.'

He was silent and I knew he was thinking about Melanie again. 'At least you're too honest and too sharp to let yourself be fooled by any emotion that isn't real ...'

'That's where you're wrong. I was prepared for years to marry a man I know now I didn't love at all, just to please our families ...' I told him about Charlie and it was a sudden ease to my guilt and pain.

All he said as I came to the end was: 'Don't you ever do that again, do you hear,' in the admonishing tones of an adult extracting a child from some hazardous adventure. He gripped my arm firmly and we looked at each other, two people who have been embarrassingly free with an exhibition of their emotions. Then he smiled, his slow sweet smile and continued in the same tone: 'Don't ever be tempted to go cave-hunting, either.' He pointed to the shadowed black holes in the cliff face. 'Some of these lead right under Priory House, so I'm told. A relic of the medieval castle.' When I said that Mrs. Miles had mentioned this he added: 'Oh yes, her husband did some excavations hereabouts. He was a historian and a well-known archaeologist.'

'Not Jefferson Miles?'

'Oh, you've heard of him.'

'So has everyone interested in local history. His books on Northumberland are marvellous. I had no idea—does Mrs. Miles really need to work? I mean, she must have a comfortable income—his books are still very popular.'

Adam shrugged. 'I guess she's like many elderly women whose families are gone and who belong to the pre-career-woman world. She wasn't trained to anything but being a good hostess and running a home is all she knows. Besides, Whitton Sands is so small, she would get very bored I expect ...'

Jefferson Miles. The name. I knew something important, a connecting link. Somewhere very recently I had seen a complete collection of his first editions. 'His speciality was the Arthurian legend, wasn't it?' I said.

'I guess so.' Adam looked surprised.

'Of course, I remember now. At Pleys Castle

Lady Ester has his books and a small museum of relics from his excavations. My school were taken round to see them. He worked on Nine-spears Crag too, didn't he?'

'Before my time.'

How odd, I thought, that the garrulous Mrs. Miles hadn't bragged once about her illustrious husband when she was ready with her entire life story at the slightest provocation.

'Well, you stay away from the caves, Julie. They're liable to collapse and we wouldn't want you entombed and drowned.'

I shuddered. 'Thanks for the warning. I have vertigo to begin with, a natural deterrent to walking up cliff-faces.' Looking around, I added: 'You're pretty well set up here for hazards, aren't you? Marie warned me on my first day not to go prancing across the moors.'

'True. The pretty green bits are marsh. Remains of the ancient moat around Whitton Castle. Keep to the main roads and you'll be safe enough. And to Priory House. It's a fortress,' he added, laughing as if the idea amused him. Again he scanned the sea, stopping occasionally to stare down at some object on the pebbled shore with narrowed darting eyes.

A searcher still, frantic for some sign, dead or alive, of Melanie. His expression reminded me of a bewildered child, who by his own dreadful carelessness has lost his most treasured possession. It shut me out and when I started to say something about exploring not seeming a worthwhile occupation with so many dangers, he murmured: 'Um?', preoccupied with his nightmare, and I felt that never again would we be close, that I had lost him.

Oh, why had I pressed on him my idiotic philosophies and told him about Charlie, instead of enjoying the light-hearted mood in which we set out to fly Hereward. Even his remark about being sensible about falling in love next time seemed a lightly veiled warning. It was too late, anyway, and I felt sickened, a born loser, as I realised each meeting, however trivial, widened the gap between the man who was Adam Hebburn and the one I had loved at first encounter.

My Horseman of Ninespears Crag was still a myth, a dream man cherished by every starry-eyed girl, who would warm to my conversation, think my words witty and admire the girl my mirror told me I could never be. The real Adam Hebburn had no lasting part—and wanted none—in the small everyday politenesses I treasured in secret. His hand on my arm, warm and strong, a tender glance, a teasing word. All

147

gave me hope of a happy ending, of love tomorrow, but in moments of cold sanity I knew they were only significant in the wild abandon of my love for him.

Life is never without surprises though. He threw the lure to Hereward who had shot skywards with shrill cries of delight, after a moment's indecision about that new tail. There was something very primitive, very close to a world long gone, in two people's delight in watching a falcon stoop to its lure, especially when the man looked like a medieval painting, his face hard, lean and strong, his eyes deepset, wide under a craggy brow ... A strange resemblance between bird and master ...

'He's made it,' said Adam. 'Good old Hereward. Just watch that grace, the way he moves, watch his instinctive use of air currents. Can't you feel his happiness, what it would be like to be a bird?'

'Oh, damn,' I said, struggling with my headscarf, for it was windy on the cliffs, 'I wish I could fly.'

Adam laughed. 'I've been wondering what was wrong with you. And what I had done to make you cross. You aren't usually quiet so long. Tired?'

'No, I'm all right,' I said, grappling with the

great length of white chiffon.

'Here, let me.' He took off the leather gauntlet, tucked it under his arm and straightened out the tangled flying ends around my neck. 'There now. Is that better?' His face was inches from my own. He said: 'You have the most beautiful eyes. That extraordinary colour belongs in the flower-garden, no human being should have purple eyes.' And I watched his smile, his face came nearer until his lips covered mine.

I couldn't even close my eyes. There on top of that windy cliffside I was incapable of speech or action. He touched my cheek. 'Your face is cold. Have I made you angry? I'm sorry. I thought you wanted me to kiss you. Sorry.' And he turned away with a little sigh.

'I did. I did.' The next moment I was sorry about the furious impulse of those words, for he put his hands on my shoulders and said: 'Julie, you mustn't get carried away.' He sounded exactly like a stern but loving uncle. 'Promise me you won't.'

'Won't what?' I asked crossly.

'You know. Get notions about me. Honey, I'm not free—and what's more I'm not worth it. You need someone your own age.'

At those familiar words I saw my newly-born

romance drain sadly away. Only men who aren't themselves in love take refuge in statements about not being free and being unworthy, the standard 'out' in every part of the civilised world.

Hereward was duly exercised in silence after that and he at least came back tired but pleased with himself. Ten minutes later we were walking down the Brandy Road as if that kiss had never been. Even his kiss had been contrived, I thought savagely, feeling ashamed of my innocence. He could see I was smitten with him and had used it as the least embarrassing way for an experienced man of the world to warn me off a tricky situation without direct unkindness. My whole life felt soured. I wanted to be sick. My legs were tired and dragged as if I had lived for ever. Perhaps I was going to die, I thought hopefully.

In the line of whitewashed cottages that made up Whitton Harbour I was glad of Mrs. Miles' shopping list as a talking point in a relationship suddenly strained to exhaustion. Adam gallantly took the post office and marched off with Hereward flapping on his wrist and making rude noises at passing cars. Then he gave a shriek of protest at being parted from me:

'Shut up,' said his master, 'she's coming back.'

I stamped into the general store. Just my luck to have a peregrine fall in love with me ...

'Right,' said Adam, when I'd finished my purchases. 'Is that everything? Cigarettes? Marie's magazines? Good.'

At the Whitton Arms an elderly man bounded straight into us. 'Hello, Adam.'

'Hello, sir.' Despite the salutations and their genial expressions, I felt both were put out at the unexpected meeting and given due warning, they normally took opposite sides of the street. The stranger's clerical collar introduced him before Adam did. Rev. Scales. Diane's father.

In appearance he had as little in common with Diane as Melanie had with Strachan. For one thing, he was a tall muscular man, who looked more suited to a military background, right down to the hearty manner and the brisk moustache. Far from the balding Friar Tuck I had imagined, cherry-cheeked and cherry-nosed, rotund. Bucolic if not alcoholic.

He beamed on me, humanly curious, and I wondered if Adam's reluctant introduction was merely embarrassment at having been so forthright about Rev. Scales' drinking habits, as he said: 'Ah, Miss Marsden, I hope you'll be happy with us. If there's anything you need, at any time, the vicarage is over there. We are all one family at Whitton Sands. Isn't that so, Adam?' His laugh seemed a trifle forced, and although my 'sharp eyes', as Adam called them, could not detect 'having drink taken', that guffaw and a sudden breeze blew a whiff of strong brew under my sharp nose.

We left him, rather quickly, I thought, exchanging mundane politenesses. Adam said: 'You seem to have impressed the parson, he'll expect to see you in church on Sunday. There's the Hebburn family pew if you're C. of E. and interested. I'm afraid keeping awake during the sermon is a necessary qualification too, as the pew is right under the pulpit. The Hebburns are rather diffident churchgoers these days. Marie used to do most of it before her accident. And Melanie too, sometimes.'

That surprised me. The picture my imagination had painted of Melanie was not of a girl praying to a Christian God. Something more pagan and mischievous. Witchcraft and Hallowe'en and moonlit churchyards, fitted the image better.

Adam was in training for taking the Brandy Road in leaps and bounds. Soon I lagged behind, breathless. We were almost at the top when he remembered me, stopped and said: 'I'm sorry. Here, give me your hand.'

Soon the hand became an arm around my waist. I was breathless and giggling, my heart racing with more than the stiff climb. A little undignified, neither of us were in any condition for a meeting with the horseman who waited patiently for us to clear out of his path.

It was Philip Riche. But today his good looks were completely overshadowed by the magnificent black horse on which he sat. It was huge, shining, rearing as impressively as any beast from a TV Western; whinnying—showing the whites of its eyes. A pure-blooded Arab stallion and a far cry from the mild-mannered cobs and hunters I normally saw trotting about the Northumbrian countryside, or the Shetland pony I had cherished but was afraid to ride as a small girl.

'Quiet, Thunder,' said Philip. He smiled at us mockingly. 'Having fun?'

'Not particularly,' said Adam. 'But I see you're enjoying yourself. You never lose your taste for the dramatic, do you, Philip?' he added, his voice cold but amused.

At his words, the horse, as if it understood, reared again, pawing the air, and I stepped back, my hand on Adam's arm, as the flaying murderous hoofs were within inches of us.

I was pleased to see that Philip had some real difficulty in controlling the horse. For a moment he looked flustered, even scared. At last he leaned over, the horse quiet, and said: 'And you, my dear Adam, never lose your taste for the romantic.' And I was blushingly conscious of his eyes on Adam's protecting arm around me as insolently Thunder's great bulk brushed us out of their path.

Adam was furious. Through the silence as we walked to Melanie's little garden I could sense his towering rage with Philip Riche and in my turn felt strangely tarnished by the encounter, as if Philip had indicated that Adam and I were having an illicit affair.

In a blundering attempt at light conversation I said: 'What a beautiful horse.'

'Damned killer,' said Adam. 'I wouldn't give him stable room, but Riche knows someone in the village.'

Killer? Of course—Melanie's horse. I remembered Diane's words when we first met that Thunder was a killer and only Melanie could ride him. I looked at Adam's face and a sudden shaft of pity welled through me for his unguarded moment of misery and humiliation.

Only his hand on my arm betrayed tenseness. Not comfort but custody. He saw me watching him and said:

'Don't mistake me, I love animals. Especially horses. But that brute threw Marie and crippled her for life.'

A car raced up the road, horn blazing. The grocer's van. Diane sprang out, shouted: 'Uncle Adam,' and raced breathlessly across towards us. Fondly she took his arm and completely ignoring my presence began an eager chat about Hereward's flying progress. I listened, bleakly out of it, feeling unwanted and somehow ill-used.

As we crossed the garden, Mrs. Miles rushed out of the kitchen, shovel in hand, looking very angry. 'Watch your feet,' she said. 'Just look at that,' and she pointed to horse droppings right outside the door. 'I've told Dr. Riche a thousand times not to bring him this way. He always drops a load right here—I'm sure he could wait till he got to the fields. I think the dirty beast does it just for spite.'

Diane said she would go with Adam to look at Starlight and as nobody asked me to go along, I followed Mrs. Miles into the kitchen, still grumbling about that 'wretched horse'. When I said we had met them on the Brandy Road, and wasn't he a beauty, she sniffed.

'Hm. Melanie's horse, if you please. Strachan gave him to her years ago. There was plenty of the gipsy in Miss Melanie. Despite her delicate looks she was as strong as an ox, and in no time she had that great brute tamed. She'd use a whip on him something awful and when Mr. Adam tried to stop her she'd say: "He's mine—my very own—but he's got to know who is his boss".' Mrs. Miles looked out of the window towards the seat where Adam had painted Melanie and her kind eyes hardened.

'She was boss all right, that horse was a devil for everyone but her. And let me tell you, Miss Marsden, beauty is as beauty does. Miss Marie had a nice quiet animal, not handsome but a little docile beast anybody could ride. One day Thunder set on him, kicked him to death—at least, he was so badly hurt he had to be destroyed.'

'It was a terrible day. Miss Marie in tears, Miss Melanie sulking. Then she said: 'You can have Thunder, I'm sick of him. He's no fun any more, too tame for me. I like horses and men with guts.' Miss Marie said she didn't want him. 'Scared of him, are you?' And Miss Melanie started to laugh. 'Oh, please yourself then, I don't care. I just wanted to stop you snivelling.' Miss Marie rushed past me and I caught her up just as she climbed over the fence. 'Don't stop me, Miley,' she said, 'I'll ride him—if he's the last horse I ever ride ...'

In the hall I heard Marie's voice, the wheelchair scrape on polished wood: 'Anyone there?'

But Mrs. Miles ignored her. 'It was the last horse she'll ever ride. Despite the doctors' assurances. Poor lass, the last horse she'll ever ride, the last fence she'll ever climb.'

I escaped as soon as I could. Up in the bedroom the wind beat hard against the windows, although there seemed only the faintest breeze in the garden. I sat on the window-seat and wondered what my parents would make of all this when I told them. I had a sudden swift vision of home, of Mum's cooking and Dad among his roses. I felt it was a long time since I had seen them—too long for me—and that I must go to Corham at once. I had worked hard and nobody could begrudge me a day off, despite the handsome salary.

My request plainly startled both Marie and Adam as we had our coffee that evening. They exchanged glances, looked troubled. That I should want to spend a day at home was clearly the last thing they expected.

And so I learned the sinister implication behind Adam's remembered words. 'You'll be safe in Priory House. It's a fortress.'

A fortress could also be a prison.

CHAPTER 8

When I announced to Marie that I wanted to go home for a visit she looked alarmed. 'My dear, is it something urgent? Your parents—they're not ill, I hope?'

'No. But I'd like to see them, and all my friends in Corham.' Surely she realised I had another life, other interests than being a dogsbody for the Hebburns? Yet her startled manner almost suggested my natural desire for home was somehow disloyal and wounding to a kind and considerate employer.

Assured that my parents were well, she gave a relieved smile and patted my hand. 'Dear Julie, I wonder would you do me the greatest favour? There's an article I simply must get off quickly. Quite frankly, I'm rather short of cash ...'

I saw little evidence of that except in fireless rooms in October. Missing central heating, a recent cold spell had sent me racing for a cardigan. Adam and Marie watched this performance in mild astonishment. No, they didn't feel it cold at all.

'A writer has to be prepared to turn her hand to anything these days,' Marie continued sadly, 'and they're waiting for this piece. Would you be a darling and go later? I'd be so grateful,' she added with a brilliant wistful smile. 'And of course, if there's anything urgent you need, perhaps Diane could get it for you. She's going to Newcastle.'

Imagination wouldn't stretch to asking Diane favours and when Marie presented me with her 'magazine piece', as she modestly called it, I was surprised by its brevity. I could have managed to type it all and still have had a weekend off quite easily, I concluded, walking back from the post-box.

Perhaps the weather contributed to my appalling home-sickness. The fine crisp autumn days brought back vividly the river at Corham and walks through the silent Roman settlement, the weeds of nearly a thousand years blowing in the wind and obliterating the still-bright mosaic floors.

Those were my first memories of my father and when I closed my eyes and sniffed the air I could imagine him by my side, tobacco smoke and all, and hear him talking, talking a blue streak as always. And the small sickness at the pit of my stomach developed into something stronger, a more urgent longing for the familiar things that were my life again. The happy tenure of every day at Corham, the bookshop with the excitement of great parcels of new books, with shining crackling covers and the smell of fresh print. A domestic scene with my favourite television programme, Mum knitting, Dad making notes for his book on *Border Badmen*. Not the exotic gun-slingers of the Wild West, but criminals who haunted the Borders of England and Scotland from the reivers to bank-robbers, murderers of modern times.

But over that cosy domestic scene there now lay an intriguing question-mark. The Marsdens weren't my parents. What tragedy had deprived me of my real mother? Who was she—and where? And did she ever wonder what had become of that baby put out for adoption so long ago?

Stop being maudlin, I told myself. This isn't a unique situation. It happens every day. And I kicked a stone with a childlike return to normality. Your yearning for home has nothing to do with the parents' revelations. You've got the grues because you're used to a good life, spoilt rotten with Mum's good cooking and a harmonious happy home. Admit it, Diane's eternal casserole and that chilly house is making you realise you'd never had it so good ...

Still, my self-analysis did nothing to prevent me uncharitably dismissing Marie's sudden head cold with a temperature that kept her in bed on the very day off I had been promised. Or Adam's sudden departure to Berwick where Grandfather Hebburn was being more awkward and wilful than usual, as deliberate attempts to keep me a prisoner in Priory House.

From the window I often watched the busy little boats rocking on a painted azure sea. There was scant evidence of their fishing in Whitton Sands, although Adam assured me that catches went to Craster for kippering. Remote and beautiful in mist, Holy Island hugged the horizon, its castle from a forgotten fairy-tale, a stage-set for an improbable melodrama with the players all gone long, long ago. Even the arch of Whitton Priory, like some great wishbone of a prehistoric monster, was out of context, belonging in a medieval painting, a lusher setting than this astringent Northumbrian landscape, all sea and blighted hill and heath.

And walking to the village I noticed again

all around the predominance of barbed wire, locked gate and warnings ... 'Don't ... Please Don't ... Strictly Private ... Trespassers will be Prosecuted ...' All rather unseemly after those glowing invitations in the guide-books, stressing Whitton Sands as picturesque, Ninespears Crag as the legendary resting-place of King Arthur, Whitton Priory as an invaluable relic to students of history.

There was something wrong, very wrong. Somehow it tied up with the Hebburns' reluctance to let me go home. I was sure I knew the reason. I hadn't much evidence as yet, but that would come. It undoubtedly lay in those fishing boats ...

Smuggling. That was it. Whitton Sands was engaged in some large-scale smuggling, probably drugs. Small packages that could be exchanged boat to boat, dropped in lobster pots— oh, there were a thousand ways in which transactions could be negotiated in safety. The more I thought, the surer I was. All those caves, the underground cellars ... Hadn't Adam told me they were once connected with the old Castle and went right to Whitton Peel itself. No wonder he had warned me off exploring ...

Perhaps there was a role for Hereward in this drama of smuggling, a package of cannabis could be dropped by appointment, disguised as a falcon's lure. Then, of course, there was Dr. Philip Riche—and I remembered triumphantly that he had been implicated in a drug scandal during student days.

But as ringleader of the smugglers my money would be on the Hermit of Whitton Peel. A character straight out of James Bond: mysterious, sinister, probably drowning his victims in the ancient dungeons, chaining them to the walls, gloating as the tide came in ...

A shadow sliced the sun away from me and a cloud loomed high over Ninespears Crag. I shivered suddenly from more than cold, and perhaps Marie mistook discomfort for sullenness, for she said as I entered the house:

'If you'd like to go home tomorrow my cold is much better. There's a bus at ten. I really should work, but it seems I'll have to go to Berwick. Grandfather is impossible just now, he gets worse each day, yet he refuses to countenance help with the farm. Really, old people can be so difficult. And not only the senile ones. The wilful strong ones only get more wilful.'

In case she changed her mind about going, I telephoned home. As the bell rang unanswered, I remembered that this was the parents' bridge evening. At the County Police Station even Police Constable Warren Browne was off duty and there was no answer from his home, either. Nothing to do but wait.

Adam returned later that evening, so that he could take Marie back with him next day. In face of Marie's protests he said: 'You know perfectly well you're the only one who can deal with him in these moods. It's true, Julie, he's always adored her,' he added with a proud look in her direction, 'even as a child she could always wrap him around her little finger ...'

'Nonsense,' said Marie.

'It isn't nonsense,' said Adam.

I took my leave, feeling that an argument was in the air and that my presence would be something of an embarrassment. As I wished them good night, I looked at my frail Porcelain Pretty employer and wondered what methods she found effective on a fierce stubborn old man like Grandfather Hebburn.

'Be sure not to miss the bus,' she said, as we met briefly at breakfast next morning. 'There isn't another until one o'clock. Adam's feeding Starlight—I wish he would hurry. He says there's a spare house-key, he'll leave it, in case you're back before us.' She was wearing a pretty fur-trimmed coat and looked gay, excited, and suddenly I wanted to see her run and skip,

165

young and happy as she should have been but for that wheelchair. And in that moment I hated Melanie for no other reason than what she had done to Marie Hebburn.

'Are your parents meeting the bus?'

'No. I want to surprise them.'

She wasn't listening, but was viewing my suitcase with some alarm. 'You won't leave us, will you, Julie? You are happy here?' she said anxiously.

'Of course I am. The suitcase is only to bring back warmer clothes.'

She gave a sigh of relief. 'I do need you, Julie, and so does Adam. You've been marvellous, quite invaluable. Heaven knows where we would get anyone as efficient again—or how long that would take.' She looked at me, smiling, head on side. 'And someone we like, who is so much on our wave-length,' she added softly.

It was just the kind of fulsome flattery quite irresistible between employer and employee. Had I intended never to return, in thirty seconds she had my promise not to forsake Priory House and to stay as long as they needed me.

Gathering a forgotten pair of shoes from the bedroom, I heard the car leave. Picturing Adam at the wheel, I wished I had said goodbye or that he had thought of looking for me before departing. It was silly to feel that every parting from him might be for ever, and an hour later, trudging up the road, I already missed him abominably. I was sorry I had been so impulsive, sure that my absence from Priory House wouldn't give him a second thought and that when I returned everything growing sweet and tender between us would be changed, with Melanie returned to enjoy my misery.

In saner moments I regarded Melanie's return as the perfect solution. It would release me from the bondage, self-imposed, of loving Adam Hebburn. The truth grew daily more painfully obvious. I had never been in love until now. I had loved Charlie Browne as childhood friend, companion, male escort, but had no feeling for him as woman for man. If I had been, instead of nervous excuses, I would have been dragging him into bed every time our parents trustingly left us alone in the house during our long courtship. Now, at last, I understood the violence of our quarrels, Charlie's incomprehensible rages, as he waited patiently but in vain for me to love him, to want him.

In the light of my treatment of Charlie my doomed love for Adam seemed poetically justified. Undoubtedly Adam was a smuggler—perhaps worse. For who was to know if Melanie ever got up in that plane? Whose word did they have except his that it was even her intention? It was the perfect alibi, if Adam had murdered her, concealed her body. Maybe he knew those caves better than he pretended, I thought grimly.

And however friendly and sweet Marie was to me, and to Adam, I could never forget the conversation I had over heard my first night at Priory House that Philip and she could 'never be happy while *he* is alive'.

I was caught up in a very nasty business indeed. Even innocent of Melanie's death, Adam was involved in some chicanery and the strange secret nature of Whitton Sands suggested smuggling.

Smugglers. Gentlemen by day, smugglers and highwaymen by night—these might well be the life-blood of the historical romances I adored, but in real honest-to-goodness twentieth-century life I saw Adam as no more than a frankly dishonest man, engaged in a distasteful occupation morally, whatever its merits financially, and *that* was one part of my theory which did not compute, as neither Hebburns seemed more than comfortably well-off.

How I wished instead he were a humble fisherman, a postman, a joiner—preferably, oh so preferably, a bachelor too.

I was learning a lot about Julie Marsden, what constituted her dreams and what she really wanted out of life. The latter undoubtedly a conventional red-brick suburban villa, with central heating, a car, a rather dull but secure husband, with a good pension scheme, and a holiday at Majorca every year. I was alarmed at how well Warren Browne fitted this role. Dear God, such is the stuff that our dreams are made of ...

I reached the bus-stop at the crossroads well in time for the Corham bus. Down below lay Whitton Sands with its red roofs. This was the road where I first met Adam Hebburn. And everything in my life before that misty night seemed part of another world, less highly coloured but infinitely safer than my present habitat. I thought of how ardently afterwards I had longed and dreamed of my Horseman of Ninespears Crag, and remembered grimly the ancient philosophy of wishes: That humans could in fact will a wish's fulfilment but they must not then blame the gods for the terrible form its gratification might take ...

I shivered. Ninespears Crag dominated the scene and through the now bare trees Whitton

Peel was cleary visible. The smugglers' head-quarters, I thought, remembering how closely it overlooked Priory House and the sea. Perhaps those curtainless windows in my bedroom were a beacon, a warning for those who rowed ashore in little boats, their oars dipping silently into a moonlit sea ...

I looked at my watch. The bus was late, the long straight road north to Berwick silent, empty but for infrequent cars passing at high speed. At last one of them stopped, going south. I thought I was being offered a lift until I saw Strachan at the wheel.

'Well, pet, what are you doing here?'

'Waiting for the bus,' I said coldly.

'You've had a long wait. It goes at nine.'

'Nine? Are you sure? Miss Hebburn said ten.'

Strachan shook his head. 'That's the summer time-table.' He opened the car door. 'You won't get another until twelve. Come on, pet, I'll take you back to the house. You might as well wait in comfort.'

I thought about refusing, decided it would be ungracious. As he leered at me, plainly aware of my discomfort, I sat as far away from him as possible and was thankful to reach the forked road to Whitton Harbour, where I asked him to set me down.

'Sure you wouldn't like some company to while away the time, hinny? How's about us having a little drink and a chat—just the two of us, eh?' The winks and grins accompanying the invitation only incensed me to decline so vehemently that I felt rather ashamed by the time I reached the kitchen door of Priory House—and discovered I had forgotten to pick up the key from the table where Adam had presumably left it. Damn. I couldn't even remember seeing a key beside my handbag as I rushed out earlier.

Well, a day that began with frustrations seemed likely to continue in them. There was nothing for it but to go down the Brandy Road, get some coffee in the village and catch the later bus, meanwhile avoiding Strachan and the Whitton Arms.

In the call-box near the vicarage I dialled the Corham number and Mum answered, apologising for the background babble. 'It's my Oxfam coffee morning.' I said I was coming home for the day, had tried to phone last night. 'Coming home,' she interrupted. 'What's wrong, dear?'

'Nothing's wrong. The Hebburns are away to Berwick.'

'Oh, well, that'll be fine, but I've nothing for lunch.' She sounded doubtful, a little alarmed.

'That doesn't matter. Good heavens, I'm not coming for an orgy, Mummy dear, it's just Dad and you I want to see. Spare the poor fatted calf,' I added cheerfully, glad she couldn't see my glum face. I wanted her to be overjoyed, excited at the unexpectedness of my visit, and there she was, merely harassed about food. 'Baked beans or spaghetti will do.'

'Oh, no,' she said, her voice shocked. 'I couldn't give you that.'

What had got into the woman? I thought miserably. Couldn't she understand that I was unhappy and needed her, not her wretched food? She was my mother. Then, bitterly, I remembered that she wasn't. Oh, it was going to take a long, long time for me to get used to that piece of knowledge I had accepted so casually on the surface.

'Shall I wait, come another day that's more convenient?' I asked, hoping my sour tone would sting her—hoping, willing her, to say: 'What nonsense, darling. We're dying to see you. It's been so long.' But she merely hm'd and ha'd as if I were one of her coffee mates wanting a fourth for bridge at an awkward time.

I said: 'I needn't come—maybe next week ...'

She said: 'Please, oh, please come,' sounding contrite. And my money gave out with only time for goodbye.

I learned something more that morning to add to my growing conviction that Whitton Sands was a smugglers' village. Visitors were not welcome. There was only one general store which sold everything, a post office, a news-agent-tobacconist which boasted an uninviting pair of rickety card tables through a beaded curtain, where one could, in dismal gloom, drink a cup of indifferent coffee. I was in desperate straits and it would have taken more than red plastic seedy table covers and chipped paint to deny my longing for a drink and a cigarette.

I had been in the shop several times before. They knew who I was and where I came from, but the hostile glance that followed my request for coffee might have indicated reluctance to bother with so small an order, or that my action was in some way unheard of, suspicious. The proprietress, an elderly woman, inappropriately named Mrs. Smiley, ignored my remark on the weather and my question about the whereabouts of Percy, her ginger tomcat who normally adorned the upstairs flat window. Normal catophiles would have responded with a rush of confidences, but Mrs. Smiley resisted the bait.

Finishing my coffee, I had a sudden brainwave. As she came with the bill, I said: 'I've forgotten my key. The Hebburns are away and I'm locked out. I wonder if Mrs. Miles would have a spare key?'

She stared at me dully. 'I don't know where she lives. They might tell you next door,' she added doubtfully.

As I waited for change, a large American car drew up outside, filling half the street. Mrs. Smiley watched it resentfully through the window, while I brooded over boxes of chocolate to see how her inhospitality coped with strangers. A large man, genial and courteous with three small children in jeans and T-shirts, crowded the tiny shop.

Mrs. Smiley received polite requests for gum and cokes in grudging silence and dismissed the child's shrill appraisal of Percy, the ginger tom, who had followed them in, with unsmiling contempt.

'I gather the inn along the street doesn't serve lunch. Any other place hereabouts where we can eat, ma'am?' Mrs. Smiley gave an abrupt negative nod. 'Coffee, then?'

'We don't serve coffee.' And *my* eyes widened at that.

'Gee, that's a pity. Make it four icicles—how about that, kids?'

While the man made a selection and eulogised about that cute old Priory, and when was it open to the public, she stared at him, grimly resisting all attempts at friendly conversation, but enthusiastically directing him on to Holy Island.

In the general store next door they couldn't recall Mrs. Miles' address. Anyway, they told me, she wouldn't be at home, she worked each day. I left sharply, banging the door behind me, their behaviour imputing truth to my sinister theory about smuggling.

Mrs. Smiley knew I worked at Priory House and greeted me civilly when I appeared with Adam. Why deny all knowledge of Mrs. Miles' address? And as I walked slowly up the hill towards the main road I remembered with a chill of anger something Mrs. Miles had told me. 'Mrs. Smiley and me—we're always being mixed up, because my first name is Sarah. A good job we live quite near each other, it's a good excuse for a cuppa when we get the wrong post.'

My cold reception in the village was quite inexplicable, for the same people were all smiles and chat when Adam was with me. Why?

And bustling down the hill came Rev. Scales. 'Good morning, Miss Marsden,' he said, shaking my hand, courtesy itself. He asked after the Hebburns, tut-tutted over Marie's cold and naughty grandpa in Berwick, frowned sympathetically at my tale of disasters, missing the bus and forgetting the key. Then abruptly, after agreeing that Mrs. Miles wouldn't be at home, he changed the subject by questioning me about Whitton Sands. Did I enjoy living at Priory House? Was it not too lonely?

He rubbed his hands with pleasure when I said Whitton Sands was a beautiful place, so picturesque, so secret.

He didn't seem to hear that, so I asked: 'What do they do here in the village, for a living, I mean?'

That baffled him. 'Well, er, they farm a bit.' I hadn't seen a farm anywhere near the village. 'And, of course,' he added, with the relieved smile of a student seeing fears die as the examination paper is well within his powers to answer, 'there's always fishing and the Priory is a great tourist attraction.'

I felt like informing him that he should have been in Mrs. Smiley's shop ten minutes ago. The National Trust would have died a thousand deaths. I also wanted to ask if any but the most desperate had ever implored the Whitton Arms for the Bed and Breakfast it advertised.

Before I could say any more, he said quickly: 'I really must be going. Parish matters, you understand. Good day.' And he hurtled along the street in the general direction of the Whitton Arms.

The American car swept past in a cloud of dust and everything was deserted. Eleven in the morning and not a sign of life in the village street. Suddenly it seemed all those little houses nestling against the cliffs, the shops, Whitton Sands itself, was a sham, a gigantic stage set raised at great cost for a film that had never been made. It was impossible to believe people were born, lived and died in those silent white deserted-looking houses, or that they fell in love or hated with passion. Perhaps already, since the 'invaders', the genial American and myself, had departed, Mrs. Smiley gave a sigh and threw aside her script, her white wig, and the storekeeper next door took off his moustache and toupee ...

At the crossroads I met a familiar grocer's van. What luck. I flagged it down and Diane leaned out, shouted: 'We've got a holiday today, isn't it super? There's a by-election and they use the school as a voting station. I'm helping Jim with the groceries. What's wrong?'

I told her I had missed the bus and she giggled, thought it a fine joke. Did she have a key?

'No, no, of course not.' But her eyes evaded me. 'You can go to the vicarage, wait there if you like ...'

I found the prospect of the empty vicarage or worse, Rev. Scales having to make stilted conversation while he longed for his bottle, quite appalling. The sun was shining on Ninespears Crag. I might never be so near again. It would be the first question Dad would ask: Had I climbed it yet? He said the view was marvellous, you could see right into Scotland; in his youth-hostelling days he had climbed it regularly.

I asked Diane how long it would take to climb and was it difficult.

'Easy, just a hill walk. You could be at the top and back in, oh, just over an hour, couldn't she, Jim?' Jim nodded silent assent, staring down the road. 'There's a path from the main road,' Diane went on, 'but that's quite a step, so we use the short cut by the back of Whitton Peel. Go in at the gate there, take the left-hand path. You'll pass the kitchen door and see a stile at the end of the garden. You go across it and keep going, to the left. You can't miss the path to the top. Here, take this, a good climb makes you hungry.' With a smile, she thrust a large block of plain chocolate into my hand. 'Cheerio, have fun.'

And before I could properly thank her, Jim started the engine and they were gone. What a pleasant friendly girl Diane was, presumably her initial dislike was mere school-girl jealousy at Adam's divided attentions. Glad to have been wrong about her after so many disappointments that morning, I was also delighted with an excuse for a closer inspection of Whitton Peel.

I opened the gate whistling, thinking how daft I had been in those first imaginings. Now it didn't look even the tiniest bit sinister, dappled in gentle sunlight. Just old, sleepy and gentle. A little nervous too, the way old houses often look, like Rip Van Winkles caught up in some other age which they can't quite understand.

I never heard the Hermit, but suddenly the grey hooded figure was there before me, taller than I had imagined him to be. I thought he was going to speak and had my apology for trespassing all ready, the calling-card my friendship with the Hebburns.

But the words were never spoken. They died

in a kind of strangled scream. Of horror. Far back in the shadowy hood, the dark hollows of eye-sockets, framed in a nasty contourless blob.

For the Hermit of Whitton Peel *had no face* ...

CHAPTER 9

My instinct to run took me straight as an arrow's flight down the side path of Whitton Peel and over the stile from Diane's directions. I was still running, choking, gasping for breath, when my feet touched the steep upward climb, little more than a sheep track leading through the heather to Ninespear Crag.

My bursting lungs couldn't take any more. I stopped, looked back. But the landscape was empty. Only the sky, the scree, the blighted moor with its swaying clumps of scrub and heather. There was no human visible, no hermit, like the hound of heaven at my heels.

I sat down thankfully, smoked a cigarette as the antidote to shattered nerves. In the distance Whitton Peel crouched, gloomy but innocent of the violence I had imagined within its walls. I thought of the Hermit again. That no-face, those empty eye-sockets. And with a sense of triumph I had the answer. Heavens, I should have been sharper at seeing the explanation;

after all, it was a favourite device in movies and in the police serial we watched so avidly at home on television each evening.

The Hermit was wearing a nylon-stocking mask. And the answer was perfectly clear—if, as I suspected, his other identity was head of the smugglers at Whitton Sands, then he had some excellent reasons for not wishing to be recognised.

I chuckled, feeling an absolute idiot. Fancy taking to heels with a yelp like a frightened pup ... I stood up and, considering the gloomy heights of Ninespears Crag, I wondered what explanation Adam Hebburn would produce for this little encounter. It would be smooth and ready, I was sure—and very, very glib ...

Suddenly I was longing to tell someone. But whom? My policeman chum, Warren Browne, would be intrigued. My parents? Certainly not my parents. If they knew their darling daughter was mixed up, however innocently, in a smuggling racket they would have a fit. And as for that sinister hermit, Mum would insist that I stay at home and I would never have the chance to satisfy my curiosity by playing Julie Marsden, Girl Detective, who, brave and true, reformed the Evil but Handsome Adam Hebburn in the very last chapter and promised to wait for him while he went to prison. I hoped for my fantasy day-dream his sentence wouldn't be too long ... I would find out discreetly from Warren how long one got for smuggling ...

Smuggling? Well, what else could it be? As I wandered along the sheep track and battled with a fierce wind not evident on the lower moorland, I had most reluctantly to admit there were some pieces of the jigsaw that didn't quite fit my theory. For one thing, the plot was all a bit too corny, right down to the missing wife Melanie, who would also turn up in the last chapter but one.

Nervously I watched the sharp cliff-face above me. Was I being too much influenced by the legend of King Arthur and his Knights sleeping beneath my feet in the depths of Ninespears Crag? For some reason that early impression of Whitton Sands persisted, that the whole village might be folded away like a gigantic stage set for a great film epic that was never made, the villagers acting parts, their lines learned ready, waiting for a cue that never came, just as King Arthur in his legend waited for the call to defend old England. And with nothing more than an intuitive flash I was sure this odd impression was somehow nearer truth than any of my wilder speculations.

Till now I had been too busy with my thoughts to notice the terrain. Except that it was bleakly uninviting. The clumps of coarse green grass, pretty at a distance, were murder to walk on, just begging for a twisted ankle. Praying that the sun wouldn't conjure snakes out of bored retirement, I stepped apprehensively through the heather, its roots bleached white, clutching the earth like fingers of long-dead men.

To the right, the ground fell away sharply, a bright smooth emerald with stone dykes and some shrubs of doubtful origin, pitifully engrossed in a gallant fight for survival against slow strangulation. Here and there, sheep stopped grazing to look down their long Roman noses in arch surprise at this rash intruder, like haughty dowagers in dirty off-white wigs. They must have given the same snotty look to Hadrian's legions patrolling Ninespears Crag, I thought, as I walked towards them and, boldness gone, they took to immediate flight, great awkward shaggy bodies on dainty legs, baa-ing blue murder, bundling into each other ...

I had the blasted heath to myself. Then I heard it. The bleating close at hand of a terrified animal. I slid down the scree, looked

184

over the dyke and there was a sheep lying on its back, struggling in vain to rise.

Well, it wasn't my day for logical thinking and had I time or inclination that morning to consult my horoscope, the stars would certainly have revealed: Do nothing on impulse. So I climbed down cautiously on to the soft green turf, making consoling noises at the frightened beast—until I found out why it didn't move.

It had more sense. I was suddenly knee deep in ooze that sucked me down with the relish and noisy lack of table manners of an unreformed cannibal. I added my human lament to the sheep's shrill despair as giant subterranean hands dragged hungrily at feet and ankles, calves and knees ...

That was just the beginning. Turning my head, I saw hovering in the sky above us a black-winged shape against the sun. A bird of prey. There was something cruel and wickedly meaningful in its lack of movement. It had probably staked out that sheep for some messy titbits, and even as I yelled again, it plummeted down from the sky.

As I buried my head, yelled at the sheep to take cover, my last thought was: One of the eagles who had attacked Hereward. Oh God. I tried to drag my legs free, shouted: 'Watch out' again, as if that silly demented woolly creature could understand.

The great beating wings cast a shadow across the sun on my back. I could feel the air move, the great claws just a whistle away. With a sob, I buried my head deep in my arms, waiting for the bird to drop beside us, the small silence of inspection before the rending of flesh and the great grisly banquet began.

'Go away!' I screamed. The beating wings continued for the eternity of several seconds, then a miraculous silence as it soared off into the sky again. 'There, there,' I said to the terrified sheep, 'that's us, safe for a while,' and to prove the prematurity of my words, the ooze grabbed me down another couple of inches. One shoe came off with a sickening plop! Then the other. The fact that they were new shoes didn't even bring a flicker of despair—I only hoped my feet wouldn't follow them.

Above the sheep, a root of heather. I grabbed and missed and seized the sheep's wool instead. It bleated shrilly, shook off my grip and I lost out another two inches of legs to the oooze. Squinting skywards into an ordeal of bright yellow sun, the blue was clear of eagles. I had some little time, and some voice still, so I yelled ...

186

There might be a shepherd, a hiker, even the Hermit would have been welcome at that moment. I knew panic would be fatal, but sickness rose in my throat, the desire to struggle and keep on struggling ... I found a small handhold above the sheep, methodically I edged towards it and after minutes that seemed to take away most of my lifetime I had regained two of the lost four inches.

Then, overhead, the dread beat of wings, the darkened sun.

I was beyond screaming, beyond hope. I slipped back into the oozing mud and prayed: Please God, don't let it be too agonising, let it be over soon ...

The wingbeat came close. It was above our heads, inches away ...

And a voice demanded: 'What on earth are you doing down there?'

I turned my head, blinking. Birds don't talk. And I saw Adam's face looking over the dyke, grinning. I would have loved him at that moment had he looked like Dracula ...

'Watch out,' I yelled, as the bird rushed at him. But he held out a wrist. It landed and I recognised Hereward.

Two minutes later, Adam had righted the sheep and it scuttled away up the hill bleating like all hell let loose. Meanwhile I was free, albeit muddied, bedraggled, shoeless, while Adam discarded his jacket, rolled up the sleeves of a pristine white shirt and dived an arm into the brown depths.

'Got them,' he said, throwing down one shoe, then the other. ' 'Fraid they'll never be the same again. Sorry.'

But I was beyond caring, savouring the beautiful relief of being safe and alive ...

Adam sat back on his heels, dangling the shoes on two fingers. 'You were a lucky girl, you chose a fairly shallow bog for your morning's mudbath. You'd have to fall face down into this one to drown,' he added cheerfully, and taking a tuft of grass, he began to tackle the disgusting mud on my legs. 'Now the other one. There, there,' he said, smiling encouragement at me, as if I were a little girl.

At being so kindly treated, idiotically I burst into tears. The next moment my head was on his shoulder and he was saying: 'Nothing to cry about, honey. You're all right. You're safe.'

'I want to go home. I want to go home.'

He patted my arm. 'There, there, so you shall. Right away.' He took out a hanky and said: 'Here, have a good blow. Better now? That's fine. Now you be a good girl and don't cry any more—I'm going to that trickle of a stream to wash your shoes. Will you be all right? O.K.?'

He went away with a cheerful backward smile, while I sniffed and stared miserably at ruined stockings and blood oozing from a cut on my leg. My skirt was ruined too. I shivered with cold, with shock and a sharp wind blowing straight from the sea seemed specially timed to add to my discomfort. The sun had vanished behind cloud and Ninespears Crag stripped of the romance of distance was a pile of old stone, menacing and sinister, older than time itself. Probably nothing more than a Pictish burial, on a natural elevation of rocks, I thought bitterly, hating poor old King Arthur for getting me into all this.

'Ka-ka,' said Hereward, nodding in agreement, perched as near me as his leather jesses Adam had anchored to a stick in the ground would allow. He put his head on the side, gave an almost human sigh of sympathy, and when I stroked his head I could have sworn that he actually chuckled ...

'So what are you two giggling about?' asked Adam, who had returned from the stream accompanied by a considerable amount of mud acquired from my dejected shoes.

'We're just having mild hysterics. You are in a mess, aren't you?'

He dabbed at a spot of moss and said: 'Nothing the cleaners can't fix.' And bending to put on my shoes, the sight of that down-bent russet head so close sent the tremor of desire stirring deep inside me. Its violence took my breath away and I knew that for good or ill I was recklessly, senselessly, in love, a love that grew stronger, less deniable, every moment I spent at Priory House.

The moment of truth was so strong I was surprised that he didn't feel something too and only said in a matter-of-fact voice: 'That's a bad cut on your leg.'

'It doesn't hurt.' There were too many other things right then for a cut on my leg to assert any priority over my bruised senses.

'That's as may be,' he said, binding a hanky round it, 'but I think we'll get Dr. Riche to take a look. Moorland bogs aren't the cleanest of places. Lots of animals—don't want you taking tetanus. Oops ...' He lifted me to my feet. 'Can you walk?'

I could and we must have made a splendid sight, Adam with Hereward on one gauntleted fist, the other arm supporting me as I limped through the heather towards the road.

When I thanked him for his timely rescue he said: 'I'm partly to blame. We left for Berwick at such a rate this morning I forgot to put the key on the kitchen table for you. That was bad enough—until Marie told me your bus time and I realised she had given you the one from the summer time-table. I came back as quickly as I could and when you were nowhere to be seen I presumed you'd thumbed a lift. However, when I was in the village Mrs. Smiley said you'd missed the bus and been in there for coffee ...'

(Kind of her, I thought. There was obviously someone she talked to.)

'... When I reached home there was old Hereward doing his nut, screaming and shrieking upstairs in the studio. I reckoned he was lonely and wanted exercise, but as soon as I released him he made straight for Ninespears Crag and ignored the lure. I thought he'd gone bolshie again—after all that trouble with the eagles, I saw him damn well losing his nice new tail ...' He stopped, looked at me. 'But it was you he was worried about. He'd seen you from the studio window. It seems incredible but with his remarkable eyesight he'd seen the whole thing and knew you were in danger.'

'And I thought he was an eagle, ungrateful

191

wretch that I am, screaming at him, trying to protect my poor lamb.'

Adam snorted. 'Your silly sheep, you mean. Anyway, he came back to me, darted about and made it all perfectly plain by his behaviour that he wanted me to follow him. Which I did, swearing about wringing his neck when I caught him. But there was our Miss Julie, the love of his life, sinking into a box, like something out of a Pearl White serial ... No wonder he looks so triumphant. Have you ever seen a smugger bird?'

We reached a stile and saying: 'Bless his dear heart,' I kissed the top of his hard feathery head. He rolled an eye at me, patently amorous and puffing out his feathers, stretched his wings in a crow of triumph and stamping his large feet in the beginning of some forgotten courtship dance, he grabbed my arm in one claw.

Adam stared. 'I've never seen anything like it. The animal behaviour boys should see this one. Good heavens ...'

'Maybe he just likes girls.'

'No. He ignores Diane and Marie—and Mrs. Miles.'

'What about Melanie?'

He looked at me stiffly as if the name was new to him and said slowly: 'He certainly didn't

192

like Melanie. In fact she was the only human I've ever known Hereward deliberately attack. Of course, she did provoke him ...' He looked at the sea, again with narrowed searching eyes in an expression I was beginning to know very well. It said plainer than words that Hereward wasn't the only one Melanie provoked either. He suddenly shook his shoulders, as if to escape that unpleasant vision, and we walked in silence for a few steps.

'Why has the Hermit got no face?' I asked.

The question took him by complete surprise, as I intended it should. After a distinct pause needed to gather wits and ingenuity, he said: 'What do you mean, no face?'

'I saw him. Close to, for the first time. He was as near to me as you are. A tall man, about your height and build, wearing that grey thing like a monk's habit. I could see his eye-sockets far back in the hood, but the rest of his face was just a nasty pinkish-white blob.'

'No face, you said?' His voice was innocently casual, as though such horrid adventures happened every day.

'That's right. Just this blob thing.'

'What an imagination you have, Julie.' But his light-hearted laugh didn't quite come off. 'What on earth did you think it was?' he added eagerly.

'After I had rushed away out of my head with terror I guessed he was wearing a nylon mask,' I said triumphantly.

Adam sighed, nodded. He was pleased by my cleverness, or somehow relieved ... 'I'd forgotten for the moment—he *does* wear a mask outside sometimes. You see, Julie,' he continued rapidly, 'he was trapped and badly burned inside a tank in the desert during the Second World War. Or so rumour has it.'

'Oh, the poor man. But why didn't they give him plastic surgery?'

Adam shrugged. 'It was too late—there were some complications by the time he was transferred to hospital. I don't know the exact clinical details—he doesn't talk about it, of course.'

I saw the whole story, the epitome of romantic tragedy. The Hermit had been a handsome, wealthy young man—he must still have money to live in what I fancied was luxurious seclusion so long after the war. He had been deeply in love with a girl who just couldn't take the prospect of living every day with this broken travesty of a face, knowing the stares, the horrified whispers at disfigurement, hideous beyond hope of resurrection.

I looked at Adam. 'Poor man. How dreadful. No wonder he retreated from the world. I expect there was some girl,' I added, eager to share my theory with him.

'I really couldn't say. I don't know anything,' said Adam. Suddenly his voice was cold, detached, forbidding further questions. He took my arm. 'It's not much farther. We're nearly home. I'm afraid you haven't a hope of the lunchtime bus to Corham.'

We had reached the steep track leading across the heather to the road at the back of Priory House. 'This is rather a roundabout way,' I said crossly. Why hadn't Adam told me in the first place that the Hermit was disfigured? Why all the mystery? He could have warned me. And I ached with shame remembering that squeal of terror as I took to my heels in the garden of Whitton Peel. Just a few words could have saved my shock and the poor man's humiliation. Really it was intolerable—why were the Hebburns and the inhabitants of Whitton Sands, always so ridiculously close about the oddest of things?

'Are you in pain or just having a happy scowl to yourself?' said Adam.

'It's rather a long way,' I said, with a bad-tempered glance back at Ninespears Crag. 'Surely the short cut would have been much quicker.'

'There isn't any short cut.'

'Yes, there is. By the side of Whitton Peel.'

'Whitton Peel. Who told you to go that way?' Adam's voice was very sharp.

'Diane told me. I met her on the road near the tower.'

'Diane? Are you sure?'

'Yes,' I said patiently. 'She was in the grocer's van and told me the quickest way to Ninespears Crag was through the back of Whitton Peel.'

'You must have misunderstood her, Julie. Diane would never direct a complete stranger that way—it can be very dangerous—as you almost found out.'

And as we stepped on to the road, the grocer's van came hurtling down. Diane leaned out, ignoring me, and beamed at Adam with a cheery greeting. Then, noticing the mud, our bedraggled appearance, she giggled: 'What *have* you two been up to?'

'Julie got immured in one of the lesser bogs.'

'Good gracious, what were you doing there?' she asked me. 'Didn't you know it was dangerous? Why, Uncle Adam, people have been sucked down ...' she added dramatically.

'I followed the path you told me to take, Diane,' I said.

She turned wide-eyed, smiling but puzzled. 'What path was that?' she asked slowly. 'When?'

At her side, Jim the young grocer's assistant, stared straight down the road like a man intent on minding his own business. I guessed there would be little use appealing to him. Feeling branded as a liar, a trouble-maker already, I said: 'When I missed the bus this morning.'

'You must be crazy,' she said angrily, cutting me short. 'I told you *distinctly* not to go near Ninespears Crag—that the moors were dangerous. I did, Uncle Adam ...' Her voice rose shrilly. 'I did, you must believe me ...'

I nodded at Jim, silent and nervous at the wheel. 'Why doesn't someone ask him? He heard you, Diane.'

Jim shook his head. 'I didn't hear anything. I was busy sorting out my orders while they were chatting, Mr. Hebburn.'

Adam frowned at each of us in turn, wondering who was wrong. Then with a strained laugh he said: 'Oh, well, let's not have a storm in a teacup over misunderstood directions.'

As though waiting for a cue, Jim started up the engine, Diane banged the van door and, darting me a furious look, murmured: 'What a nerve.'

We watched them go. Storm in a teacup, misunderstood directions. A pack of lies ...

'You must be tired,' said Adam, mistaking anger for weariness. 'You wait here and I'll bring the car. I want Dr. Riche to have a look at that leg and it's a fair step to the village. Shall I ring your parents and tell them you've been delayed?'

I turned away as he hurried down the road, furious with everyone. With my mother for her indifference to my homecoming, with Marie and Adam Hebburn for their forgetfulness about the key—forgetfulness was doubtless bewitching in artistic temperaments but it had landed me in a fine pickle. But most of my anger was with Diane. Why had she deliberately lied and sent me into danger?

With a cold chill of fear, I remembered that she was still a child in years. Fifteen. Surely not intentionally wicked, perhaps more a child's senseless practical joking. Mischievous or wilful. The words conjured up Mrs. Miles' description of Melanie. Melanie who could tame wild horses yet provoke a gentle peregrine like Hereward to attack her ...

I looked at the grey secret sea, unable to believe that she was dead, that some day her body would be recovered from the sea and the unquiet nerves of Adam Hebburn would be at rest ...

Perhaps, I thought, watching Adam's white car nose out of the gate of Priory House, that story about the lost airplane was very convenient. Perhaps someone weary of provocation had silenced the teasing, the mischief for ever.

Or was Melanie biding her time and, when everyone was happy, waiting to spring out and tear their rebuilt lives to shreds?—The October Witch with a vengeance ...

CHAPTER 10

Dr. Philip Riche's domain was something of a surprise. A small ugly yellow semi-detached, one of four built in an economical but determined onslaught of modernity fifteen years earlier. But modernity had no place cheek by jowl with the ancient picturesque street of whitewashed cottages, and rosy expectations of a trade revival never materialised. So building was abandoned and Whitton Sands reverted to its sleepy past, to old dreams of smugglers and in recent times the more respectable fame of kippers. Until disaster came and the great offshore herring shoals, obeying some strange natural law of the underseas, vanished and took Whitton Sands' great trade boom with them.

Watching the gentle silver waves ebb and flow like a pattern of crochet lace on the pebbled beach, now silent, once echoing to the swirl and dive of seagulls following the herring fleet into the tiny harbour, I wondered what secret industry had taken its place? There was a fine unrestricted view from Dr. Riche's un-prepossessing front door, with its peeling paint and gloomy windows, their sad net curtains yellowed and neglected. I felt oddly discom-forted, the reason doubtless that patients are subconsciously soothed by lusher evidence of the medical professions's opulence. Even at home in tiny Corham our doctor had a great grey Victorian house with neat lawns sloping down to the river, boasting calm airs of furni-ture polish and antiseptic prosperity.

Dr. Riche's door lacked name-plate and in-dications of surgery hours. Having impatiently rang the bell twice, I decided that however this young man earned a living, the National Health Service contributed little to it. Almost relieved that he wasn't obviously at home, I looked hopefully at the car by the pavement where Adam stared straight ahead, ignoring my silent plea, his thoughts his own.

'I'll wait,' he had told me. 'I have, er, per-sonal reasons for not meeting Riche. We're not on particularly good terms.' So much had been obvious from that meeting between them on the cliff-top, with Thunder prancing danger-ously, and adding his own special touch of drama. 'However, despite my feelings, he's a darned good doctor.'

That wasn't immediately apparent. After his initial shock at seeing me on his doorstep, doubtless believing I was there with some secret message from Marie—until he noticed Adam sitting tight-lipped in the car—the glum sulky look settled back on his handsome face and somewhat reluctantly he showed me into what he called the surgery. A dismal almost empty room, furnished third- or fourth-hand, I suspected, with an old-fashioned dispenser's cupboard and a shabby divan, presumably filling the role of what my Corham doctor loftily called the examination couch. There was tattered brown lino on the floor, all evidence of pattern long since faded and everything looked depressed, seedy and hard-up, his degree in a frame under a cracked glass ...

But Adam had been right about one thing. Despite my first unfavourable impressions, the hands that examined my leg, ankle and foot were professional and efficient, the hand steady holding the syringe for the anti-tetanus injection.

'It's not deep enough for stitches,' he said, 'the plaster will pull the edges together. Should heal in a couple of days, come back if it doesn't.' He worked silent, almost suspiciously, with no disposition towards idle chatter and showing me out with brusque rapidity, he gave Adam's profile a hard angry glance and slammed the door behind me.

As Adam negotiated the steep bend, I said: 'It took him longer to open the door than to attend to me.' Adam was not to be lured. 'Does he have another job?'

'Of course not. Why should he?'

'It doesn't look like a thriving practice, that's all.'

'He has enough patients, I imagine,' said Adam, staring carefully ahead.

'Enough to run a car and a horse like Thunder? But the house is so down-at-heel, his housekeeping looks well below par.'

Adam chuckled. 'I see Sharp Eyes have missed nothing.'

'Well, it's hardly Tannochbrae in there.'

And Adam came, quite surprisingly, to Philip Riche's defence. 'Of course it isn't. Why should it be? People in small villages expect their doctor to visit them.'

That was a lie. Another one, I thought coldly. Almost as big a whopper as Diane's, when she denied all knowledge of directing me to Ninespears Crag, via the short cut through Whitton Peel.

The car swung into the drive of Priory House

and I thought of it being empty. For the first time I would be alone there with Adam. I felt excited and a little embarrassed, hoping he would kiss me again and knowing I would respond like a greedy child. The consequences of such behaviour, of encouraging him, took my mind to thoughts of wilder passion, for I knew that whatever he suggested, I wouldn't be capable of even a token resistance.

But, alas, my virtue was never in danger. If I had used my head even tolerably well I should have known Marie would be back too. He could hardly leave her in Berwick. At her smiling face I felt a moment's unreasonable, quite uncharitable, anger, as she held out her hands to me, all apologies.

'Julie dear, what on earth must you think of us? Oh, your poor leg. It could all have been avoided. With Mrs. Miles so near it's her day at Whitton Peel. She would have come over and let you in ...'

Was that why everyone refused information about Mrs. Miles? Because callers weren't welcome at Whitton Peel. It was making some sense.

So Mrs. Miles, highly respected historian's widow, had a part in this mystery too ...

Preoccupied, I listened more glumly than was

in keeping with politeness and my silence was misinterpreted. She put a timid hand on my arm.

'I'm such a silly, do forgive me. When one doesn't use buses personally, you know ...' That slight helpless gesture and sad smile wrung my heart. God, I had two strong legs to walk on, to run and dance—was I selfish enough to make a world issue of missing the bus and getting a scratch on my leg? '... the new time-tables are here. Would you like to go tomorrow?'

'I'd still rather go today, if it's all right. May I phone home?'

Marie looked injured. 'Adam has spoken to them already. He arranged that you should go tomorrow.'

What a cheek, I thought. He might have told me he was being so busy on my behalf. 'Well, I'd rather go today,' I said firmly, and looking at the time-table. 'There's a bus at four.' I excused myself, and dialled the Corham number. 'Dad? I'm furious ...' I began.

'Never mind, pet. Mum will be pleased. She's got something nice in for your tea,' he added soothingly, as if my only reason for coming home was Mum's tempting cookery.

I changed, had a quick shower and from the bedroom saw Adam trotting Starlight towards the moor. For once I didn't care that we wouldn't say goodbye. I was going home and it suited me fine to be rid of his unnerving presence and its effect on my usually well-regulated emotions.

Declining Marie's offer of tea, I reached the bus-stop in plenty of time. But staring down the empty road a kind of deadly fatalism overcame me. It seemed all too easy. The bus wouldn't arrive and I was a prisoner behind some invisible barrier which cut Whitton Sands off from the rest of the world. Even the weather had changed and the bright day vanished in a leaden overcast sky with a chill wind blowing straight from Cheviot. Far below the village brooded over a flat sea. In this suddenly lifeless landscape I knew again the unreasoning upsurge of terror I recognised from that first occasion when I was stranded in the mist. Surely it had been an instinct that all was not well ...

An instinct for danger ... Anxiously I consulted my watch. Five minutes late, what *was* I to do? And at that very moment the bright yellow bus came trundling down the road. Overjoyed, I seized my case ...

But long before the bus reached me it was overtaken by a white car driven fast. It slithered to a stop beside me.

Adam opened the passenger door. 'Get in. I'll give you a lift.'

'To Corham?' I said, amazed. He nodded, muttered something I missed, lost in the vibration as the bus roared past us. He followed it for twenty yards, then stopped, reeled down the window, poked out his head and did a three-point turn. The next moment we were thundering back towards Whitton Sands.

'I thought you were taking me to Corham?' I said angrily. 'You said you were giving me a lift.'

'And what else is this but a lift?'

I could have wept. 'You idiot. I was going home tonight. The parents are expecting me.'

'All right, all right.' He smiled. 'I've taken care of all that. Marie told me when I came in, so I phoned them. They tell me Wednesday's the shop's half-day, so I invited them here instead, for lunch.'

'Honest?'

He chuckled. 'What do you mean, "honest"?' And his face suddenly solemn. 'Why should I trick you, Julie?' I shrugged, muttered that I didn't know and he said, 'Well now, aren't you pleased?'

'Of course,' I said doubtfully. 'They'll love Priory House.'

Marie clasped her hands like a small child offered a sudden, unexpected treat. Excited, delighted about my parents' visit, her tizzy over menus for the occasion was more appropriate to one entertaining royalty. It was rather sweet and oddly pathetic, I thought, this anxiety to make an impression on a simple North Country bookseller and his wife.

I went to bed early that night, my sleep accompanied by some muddled nightmares in which my parents didn't arrive ... And one thing was very, very clear. Something I didn't dream at all but *knew* with absolute sanity. Whether I liked it or not, this visit of my parents was merely to lull my suspicions—and theirs, if any. I was a prisoner in Priory House. Someone was determined I shouldn't leave it— alive.

And the word 'alive' came like a sombre whisper as I thought of the missing Melanie ...

We were to have a late lunch for my parents' benefit. Helping Marie in the kitchen, I felt my festive air was rather out of proportion, belonging to kin welcomed home from overseas rather than parents last seen two weeks ago and forty miles away. And because my joy was so great I wanted to 'rap wood' over it all. Yet surely this visit would put my fears finally at rest. In broad daylight, rolling pastry in a busy kitchen, it was quite idiotic to believe that I was somehow a prisoner in this charming house at the hands of such a delightful couple.

I ran through to the hall many times, imagining I heard a car and each time came back bleakly aware of disappointment and foreboding. The clock struck two, Marie sighed and said: 'Everything's ready, Julie,' and at that moment, making nonsense of my nightmares, I heard the familiar 'peep, peep' of Dad's car. The next moment it seemed I was in Mum's arms, our eyes full of outrageously sentimental tears. Then Dad was kissing me, laughing: 'Hello, Julie love.'

And uncaring that an amused Adam towered over this little domestic scene, we all stood there in the hall, gabbling at each other. The importance of the 'occasion' gauged by Mum's obviously recent visit to the hairdresser—a stylish coiffure enhanced by a frivolity of hat, took ten years off her. There was more care with makeup, too, than her usual 'dash of lipstick and a dab of powder'. Eyebrow pencil and eyeshadow were in evidence.

Not to be outdone, Dad, wearing one of his hated lounge suits instead of comfortable corduroy jacket and sweater, showed unmistakable signs of a very recent hair-cut. They followed Adam and me reverently from room to room, clearly charmed and honoured to be shown over the home of Adam Hebburn, the artist. I could see Mum storing up mental notes for her bridge chums ...

In the drawing-room conversations slid along —over Marmion and Holy Island, the local history bringing a gleam to Dad's eye. And while Adam attended to our pre-lunch sherries I watched them closely—and in dismay. They looked like my parents, talked like them, behaved in identical fashion, Mum playing with a mole on her chin as always when she was nervous; Dad drumming long fingers silently on the arm of his chair. But despite all the familiar signs, these people were strangers.

Strangers. And as if my thoughts electrified the air, there was a sudden hush in conversation while they both turned, stared at me uncomfortably. Then Adam, taking it as a signal to refill glasses, jumped to his feet and Mum, shaken back to normal giggles, said: 'No thanks, I'd better not ...'

'How's Lady Ester?' I asked.

And all three froze. If I'd asked after Mao Tse-tung himself they couldn't have looked more surprised.

'Lady Ester?' I repeated, and Dad came down to earth with a jolt that almost sent his sherry flying.

'Fine, fine,' he said, and Mum's nervous gulp was clearly audible. I turned to look at Adam, who was standing behind the settee, and something shadowy that had been haunting my mind, an elusive something which had bothered me since we first met, clicked into place.

In a fairly poor light Adam Hebburn could have passed for a young Hector Pleys. The resemblance lay in the turn of his head, a gesture, for he was by no means as handsome, his features quite different. No, he wasn't really like him at all, I decided, except in that fleeting way, height and build too. I concluded that I would never have noticed it if Hector's aunt, Lady Ester, hadn't been in my mind and had triggered off a chain reaction of associations.

I knew I couldn't tell him. He would think I was flattering him, that I was one of those silly females who see resemblance to television or film stars in everyone. I sipped my sherry thoughtfully. Still, it was a strange coincidence and I wondered if, when he painted Hector Pleys as King Arthur—himself twenty-five and Hector over forty (before his tragic death on location in Africa)—was the resemblance already there? Or was it a growing likeness? Had Adam, liking and admiring Hector, unconsciously modelled himself on the older man? And I wondered if the ageing actor had looked at the young artist with envy and saw in Adam, himself in a distorted mirror, as once he had been before youth was lost ...

Around me, the conversation had swerved back to that safe topic, painting. Over lunch where Marie and Mum found a common interest in gardens, Adam entertained Dad to the mysteries of texture, balance, perspective, his enthusiasm denoting the hard-working painter. I listened, remembering the wearied sketchbooks, the deserted studio which Hereward now occupied, his perch staring across the moors. I thought of paint tubes hardened with disuse, his pallid illustrations of wild flowers for Marie's book, and how it all fitted my theory that his pose as painter was a convenient mask for other activities. Cynically amused at the admiring respect on my father's face, the gratification on my mother's, I wondered how they would react if they knew their daughter had been left in the custody of a man whose real living was earned by smuggling.

And when at last, with a theatre date to keep

with friends in Newcastle, they made preparations to depart, I knew that more than anything else I wanted to go back to Corham, to cling to them and the safe happy life we had enjoyed before I met Adam Hebburn.

In the bedroom that had been Melanie's, Mum sat at the mirror, fondly touching silver-backed brushes and arranging her new hat. She said: 'Cheer up, Julie pet. What's wrong?'

And I longed to say: 'Mum, I'm crazy about Adam—haven't you noticed? I'm going mad, I love him so much.' But she would have looked shocked and embarrassed at this display of intimate emotions from her usually sensible daughter, so I said: 'I'm homesick—I'd like to come home with you.'

Tucking in a tendril of hair, she said: 'Well, why not? If Miss Hebburn can spare you. We could drop you off on the way ...'

I put down a silver brush with a bang. 'I mean *home* for good.'

In the mirror her eyes met mine. 'Oh, you can't mean that, dear,' she said in a hushed voice. 'Why, it's such a lovely house. Aren't they kind to you?' she looked round and sighed. 'They've given you this lovely room too. They must think highly of you ...'

'The room belongs to Adam's wife,' I said

savagely.

'Ah, yes, the poor thing. What a tragedy,' she whispered. 'It was all in the papers.' She fastened the collar of her coat. 'Not, mind you, that I approve of women gallivanting about like that.' And gallivanting in Mum's language meant going around with other women's husbands instead of working off their craving for excitement in a Continental recipe or a pair of new curtains. 'In my day it was considered very fast, but they *seem* such nice people,' she added doubtfully. For 'nice' I read famous, wealthy—things that would give the dear soul vicarious pleasure in telling her friends Julie was secretary to the writer Marie Hebburn, whose brother Adam was a famous painter. No one could blame her for that, but I was hurt that she didn't even ask if I were happy, which I felt should have been her first consideration.

She misunderstood my silence. 'Why do you want to leave, dear?' she asked gently. 'Is it Warren? Do you miss him terribly?'

'Hell, no. Sorry, Mum. No, I miss you and Dad, and sometimes I feel like a prisoner here,' I ended rapidly.

Mum's eyebrows raised. 'A prisoner? Surely not, dear, there are buses pass the top of the road.'

'With plenty of barbed wire in between.'

She looked at me and laughed, but there was a kind of wild hysteria that I recognised from other times of stress. She patted my hand. 'Barbed wire, indeed. There's that overripe imagination at work again.' When I didn't smile she said sternly: 'I think you should stay a little longer, if they need you. After all, you can't let Miss Hebburn down when her book's almost finished.'

'She said just for two weeks.'

'Of course she did, but it's taking longer than she thought. She was so apologetic to Dad, about keeping you from the shop, but I told her not to worry because I like working in the shop again. Oh, she's such a dear, Julie, and so helpless—it just breaks my heart to see her. Don't let her down.' I didn't answer and she continued rather coldly: 'I know it's your business and you must please yourself, but how I'll ever face Lady Ester again ...'

So that was it. The lady of the manor must not be offended. I was about to protest at this return to feudal splendour when she gave me a sly glance and added the *coup de grâce:* 'And that poor Mr. Hebburn too, with this awful tragedy. She was saying what a great comfort you are to her brother too.'

A comfort to Adam. Snatching eagerly at crumbs of hope, this appeal to my better nature finally persuaded me to stay. A comfort to Adam. Well, well.

Dad and he were waiting in the hall, and as we said goodbye, Adam followed them into the garden: 'I'm taking your parents for a quick look at the Priory,' he said.

Dad looked pleased. 'Haven't seen that Crusader's Tomb for years.'

'Don't die of fright, then,' I said. 'The first time I met Adam standing by the arch, I thought the old Crusader had come back to life.'

'I'll come in your car, if I may,' said Adam. 'It's no distance to walk back.'

'Hold on, I'll come too,' I said. And at once the feeling of closeness to my parents, slowly regained through the hours, vanished. As they exchanged nervous glances, I was looking into the faces of strangers. I intercepted Adam's quick smile at his sister, over my head, and she said:

'Julie dear, I almost forgot in all the excitement. There's one letter—really quite short, but important. I'd like to have it typed and in this evening's post. You don't mind, do you?' she asked my parents.

216

They said no, gave me a final hug and darted into the car. As I waved from the step I wondered why was everyone behaving as if there was a plane to catch? Why couldn't they have waited until I typed the letter and we could have all gone to the Abbey together?

Ten minutes later, Marie appeared full of apologies. 'What a nuisance—I won't be able to send that letter, after all, Julie. It needs an enclosure, I find. What a pity.'

She wheeled herself into the kitchen and I seized my coat from the cloakroom, impelled by an odd determination, a kind of fury that because for some reason I wasn't wanted I was damned well going. As I ran up the road, I noticed Dad's car wasn't there and concluded he'd taken it along the steep lane. But the lane was empty. Still I hurried, reached the ruined arch and listened. No voices. Nothing but the sea birds, calling in the darkening sky, while the Crusader slept on undisturbed, his face like a blackamoor's, black and shining, in the sudden heavy shower. My coat was wet but I hadn't even noticed the rain ...

Feeling angry and frustrated, I surveyed the landscape from the top of an old abbey stone. They must have changed their plans, and I expected from this vantage point to see Adam walking down the road.

Then I saw how they had changed their plans indeed ...

Even as I watched, Dad's car nosed its way cautiously out of the gate of Whitton Peel. Mum and Adam had a few moments' conversation, then she got in beside Dad and Adam with a brief wave vanished back into the garden.

And suddenly I was remembering an incident that had worried me all afternoon. When I was bringing crisps for the sherry from the kitchen I dropped some from an overloaded dish just outside the drawing-room door. As I leaned over to gather them up, I heard Adam ask distinctly and rather irritably: 'Why the devil did you tell her? Was it absolutely *necessary?*'

By the time I opened the door, there were smiles everywhere, but Dad was biting his lip and Mum looking rather flushed.

The episode puzzled me. Adam's peremptory tones, bad-tempered as he was sometimes with Marie and Diane, were quite out of keeping with the courtesy he showed to stranger like the Marsdens. And often in the days that followed my parents' visit I longed to ask him what he thought it was unnecessary that I should have been told, and already waiting when I returned from the Priory, how he had walked back from Whitton Peel without a spot of rain on him, while I was completely drenched?

Mum usually phoned on Sunday evening for a 'long chat' in the cheap time. I looked forward to hearing from her that week. Nothing had happened that could be regarded as suspicious—except that I still felt like a prisoner. Watched over, protected, but a prisoner, just the same.

When the phone rang I dashed to the study, but Adam was already there. 'Hell, yes ...' Covering the mouthpiece, he whispered. 'It's for me.' But two minutes later, although I hadn't heard a second ring, he called: 'Telephone for you, Julie.'

It was Dad. Mum had flu and was very poorly. Could I come home for a day or two? Mr. Hebburn had said it would be all right ...

CHAPTER 11

Prepared for yet another doomed journey, I dreaded the walk up the steep road past Whitton Peel to wait for a bus that in nightmare never arrived. This time, however, Adam regarded my mother's illness as alarming and insisted on driving me home.

I greeted his decision with dismay, regarding this suspicious generosity as a prelude to some last-minute excuse he, or Marie, were contemplating to detain me in Priory House. But Marie in her wheelchair beamed and anxiously hoped I would find all well at home. Full of misgivings, I drove off at Adam's side, preoccupied for several miles with the shape imminent disaster might take. Slow puncture? Engine trouble? Even a corny 'out of petrol' wasn't entirely to be dismissed. Adam talked little, apart from conventional enquiries about my comfort. He drove fast with the ease and confidence of a man who enjoys speed for its own sake.

As Corham drew nearer, I relaxed and took secret pleasure in being so close to him, in the physical contact of arm and shoulder as the car swung round corners and glided across hills like a great white bird. I looked lovingly at the long narrow head with its high-bridged nose, stubborn chin and wide deep-set eyes, their piercing look so reminiscent of the peregrine Hereward, a reminder of the old saying that owners grow to look like their pets. A bird of prey. He would like that, I thought.

Certainly he didn't remotely resemble the actor Hector Pleys in profile. That fleeting likeness I had observed when my parents were visiting Priory House was surely general physical type, height and build alone. I decided I must mention it to him, nevertheless. Some day, some time more opportune, when surer of his affection, he wouldn't think mere flattery was intended.

It was already dark with lights glistening along the river walk and the Abbey church lit for choir practice when we reached the outskirts of Corham. The journey safely over, we were outside No. 16 The Cloisters and Adam had negotiated the obscure lane without any help from me.

He switched off the engine, turned round and

221

smiling laid his arm across the back of my seat. 'This is it, Julie. Hope everything's okay in there. Give your folks my regards—and let me know when you're ready to leave. I'll come and collect you.'

'Please don't trouble. I'll get the bus.'

'No, you won't. Buses are treacherous things. They don't turn up sometimes,' he added, with an impish smile, as if fully aware of my suspicions. 'Understand?' he said, tapping my shoulder gently. 'I don't want to lose you. *I* want you to come back to Priory House. You won't let me down, will you, Julie?'

'No—of course I won't,' I stammered.

Smiling, he leaned forward and, tipping my face towards him, he kissed me very gently on the lips. 'That's understood, then. Good night, Julie.'

Still with the touch of that warm mouth, dizzy, delighted, bemused, I got out of the car. It sprang into life, began to pull forward. 'No—not that way,' I shouted. 'It's a cul-de-sac.'

Still smiling, he reeled down the window. 'I know. I know. There's a drive at the end where I can turn. Take care ...'

I waited until the car passed by again to wave to him. I had the gate open and was running down the path when I realised something very odd indeed. Tucked away on a modern estate, most people find the location of The Cloisters, so inappropriately named, quite baffling, yet he had negotiated the narrow street and the difficult cul-de-sac turn effortlessly. As the houses were new, the chances of Adam Hebburn knowing any of the other five families seemed remote.

Only my parents, whom he had apparently met for the first time last week at Priory House. And as I let myself into the hall, I wondered how many times before he had called secretly at this house, and on what mysterious business?

Dad rushed to greet me. He didn't ask about Adam or how I had got home so quickly, his only concern was Mum, whom the doctor had put on to antibiotics. She looked pale and strangely childlike with her long hair spread over the pillow.

During supper Dad mentioned that Warren was in Newcastle at a police course. I was glad, hoping only that I would be away from home again by the time he returned. Warren was the final straw to my emotional complications and I always imagined him poised ready to propose the moment I relaxed my 'jolly good chum' manner with him.

By next morning, Mum was a little better

and soon I was busy about the house, tying the familiar red-checked apron she had bought me at a Women's Institute bazaar, peeling potatoes with an old broken-down kitchen knife we had used for years, staring into the pantry at the King George VI Coronation mug Dad got at school beside a cracked unusable milk jug, kept because there was a matching sugar-basin. In like manner, cups without handles were optimistically kept and twice a year Mum carried the invalid contents of the pantry on a determined foray around the Newcastle sales, but they remained unmatched.

Mum's state of mind wasn't helped by being married to an arch procrastinator who saw himself as the original home handyman and quite undefeated by tasks meant to defy any amateur. Through the years we had accumulated strange treasures—'too good to throw out'—table lamps without switches, now merely ornamental, electric fires without fuses and in the base of the pantry a toaster, one of two Charlie and I had been given as an engagement present. Its presence was a constant reproach to Dad, who cheerfully maintained that he'd 'get a new element and fix it when he had a minute'.

Seeing that toaster brought back Charlie so

clearly. Charlie. I leaned against the door, thinking of him, feeling ashamed that so long, so many days slipped by now without me giving him a single thought.

'Dead but not forgotten.' How hopeful seemed that epitaph in forlorn overgrown churchyards. And the heart wept, the senses cried at how much more often it meant: 'Dead and soon forgotten.'

In the past Dad possessed some uncanny gift of reading my mind. The day I baked was no exception. He said: 'Charlie's mother was asking after you. I thought if you had time ...'

'Now how did you know that?' I said.

He smiled. 'Lass, you were standing there with such a load of misery on your face. It wouldn't take a mind-reader to guess that home reminds you of poor Charlie. Why do you think your mother and I were so glad, so happy to see you away to a new life for a while?'

'But I love being home, honestly.' I hugged him, tears in my eyes, and he looked embarrassed, so I asked: 'How's *Border Badmen* going?'

'I've done some work on it,' he said proudly, 'but it's more fun with your help. You're better at sorting out than I am—if you have time?'

'I'll take it up to bed with me, read over your notes.'

'That'll be great. Thanks, pet.'

But that night I was too tired as I went to bed in my own familiar room, relieved that this so-normal house made nonsense of my fears. Yet as I fell asleep I wondered about my parents, the Marsdens. Wondered what was the connection with Adam's tones of familiarity to them when he thought I was out of earshot at Priory House and how he knew the exact location of this house, even in the dark.

Suddenly I felt slightly sick as a new idea occurred to me. In the cliché of those old gangster movies resurrected with such regularity on television did Adam Hebburn have something on my parents? Was my innocent-seeming book-loving dad in the smuggling game too? Was I unknowing hostage at Priory House as insurance that the Marsdens behaved themselves?

The note of pleading in Mum's voice—'just a little while longer'—took on a new significance, a horrid desperation. That day at Priory House when I had begged her to let me come home and their visit had ended with a strange secret call at Whitton Peel ...

Two days later Mum was sitting up in bed,

moping about what was going on in her kitchen, how many dishes had been broken and pans burnt black?

'I see you've recovered,' I said, delighted and amused at this speedy return to bossy efficiency. Fluffing up her pillows, I promised her some glossy mags and a box of her favourite chocolate mints when I went to Corham.

As I walked down the hill at nine that morning, the Tyne gleamed in late autumn sunshine. Beyond it the ancient pattern of two civilisations still endured. The huddled broken outline of the Roman town that Hadrian built. The fat stolid shape of the medieval Abbey, patched here and there but still magnificent. And beyond river, fields, the sharp clear outline of hills. By narrowing my eyes and using a little imagination, I could fancy Ninespears Crag among them. Ninespears Crag and Adam Hebburn, both waiting for me. And I was overwhelmed by a frenzied longing to return to Whitton Sands.

Shopping in the village became a royal progress. The kind hospitable people I had known all my life continually pressing small gifts into my hands for Mum, for myself, concealing generosity behind brusque manners and stern unsmiling faces which forbade too much sentiment displayed in excessive thanks.

I loved them all. I loved my home, but, alas, I was part of this tranquil Corham life no longer. My past as Julie Marsden, the girl who was going to marry poor clever handsome Charlie Browne who was killed, and my present—someone who wasn't a Marsden at all and was tied up in some baffling secret game at Whitton Sands she couldn't begin to fathom —would never quite meet again.

The Browne farm was only a mile distant. Carrying my parcels and some flowers, I walked deep in my own problems and the car shot past, slithered to a halt and hooted twice before it got my attention.

'Julie, what are you doing home?' Warren, Charlie's elder brother, his policeman's uniform very becoming, his face—without being handsome—honest and attractive. Small wonder the Corham girls all sighed over him, I thought.

'What a surprise. Nobody told *me* you were home again.' His voice was accusing but pleased too. 'Are you back for good?' And without waiting for a reply: 'I never thought you'd stay in that God-forsaken place this long. Going up the road? Hop in.'

He looked glum as I explained that my return was only temporary, till Mum was better. 'I thought I might look in and see your mother.'

His broad grin showed how glad he was that the suggestion had come from me and I wondered, conscience-stricken, how much speculation my non-appearance had with the Brownes. How much was written off sympathetically, for the sorrowing bereaved fiancée who had fled from constant reminders of what-might-have-been. And how much for 'that strange lass, Julie. Always was a bit hoity-toity. Not like the rest of us.'

'I've a call further on. I'll come back for you.'

'Trouble with poachers?' I asked. Warren grinned. It was a joke in the village that poachers had a monopoly on Corham crime.

He stopped at the farmhouse door. The next moment Mrs. Browne was hugging me to her ample pinafored-bosom, scooping up newspapers, rearranging cushions and trying to make an immaculate room impossibly neater.

'Such a mess it is. And I've been up since six.'

I sniffed the air. The cottage had its own particular smell which struck a chord of sadness, a yearning for the safe long-ago. And watching Mrs. Browne make tea, smiling at me so often and so tenderly, I thought with love that perhaps my main reason for wanting to marry her son was to have had such an easy mother-in-law as this.

But when we sat down together and I had exclaimed with delight over home-made scones and jam, the conversation turned to impersonal topics and stumbled as constantly her eyes wandered to Charlie's graduation photograph on the mantelpiece. Sadly I recognised that without him there was little common ground left for either of us. For a while we retreated into the past:

'Do you remember the Sunday School party nearly twenty years ago when my Charlie came home and said he was going to marry Julie Marsden, because she had purple eyes, like pansies.'

'Do you remember the day we had that family outing and Charlie and I got chased by the Chillingham white cattle?'

'The day the ice on the river broke and you nearly drowned but the two lads pulled you out, Charlie claiming he'd saved you and Warren insisting you'd both have drowned if it hadn't been for him?'

'Charlie's graduation day in Durham. Remember how it rained?'

As I remembered with a fixed smile on my face the past was becoming more unreal and nightmarish. Like listening to someone else's life story, a dull and rather boring girl, not even particularly likable. And I wondered how at any time I could have cheek enough to think I might have turned into a farmer's wife, or deserved a nice fellow like Charlie Browne.

And worse, as Mrs. Browne talked, starry-eyed, wiping away the occasional tear, I remembered with agony how I had been what Mum would call 'a *good* girl' and the hypocrisy of chastity that was easy becuase it wasn't really love at all.

Then I realised something had caught my wandering attention. She was asking me if I had met Diane Scales? 'Mervyn Scales, her father,' she said proudly, 'is a remote relative, on my mother's side. The poor man, he used to be vicar of Corham, but he hit the bottle badly after his wife died when Diane was a bairn. You wouldn't remember that.' She shook her head sadly. 'Aye, he was a good preacher and popular too. You don't get them like that now in the Abbey Church. All this high Anglican stuff, I don't hold with it at all ...'

Warren arrived. I kissed her dear worn face. 'Come again, lass,' she whispered. 'Will you? It's been like a tonic seeing you.'

'I'll come again,' I promised.

'You really cheer Mum up so much,' said

Warren approvingly, as we drove away. 'She broods a lot. Charlie was always her favourite,' he added without resentment, and I winced with shame at my selfishness. What was an hour of tortured conscience if it gave his mother happiness?

'I'll go more often,' I said, and meant it.

Warren stared at the road and cleared his throat. 'It doesn't hurt you now—I mean, remembering Charlie?'

'Of course it doesn't.'

He gave me a long deep look and said softly, 'I'm glad, Julie. I'm glad of that.' And when he pressed my hand I realised my fervent honesty had been misinterpreted. Warren probably now thought I was seriously considering him and waiting for that proposal.

Hastily I changed the subject to our various friends. Warren answered my questions who had got engaged, had quarrelled, was going with someone else and I listened in dismay. Once I had known, felt close to these friends who made up 'our set', now even their names seemed unfamiliar, their faces a blur. And I realised how ill-equipped a short time at Whitton Sands had left me to take up the threads of my old life at Corham again. With an almost physical ache, I longed for Adam.

Then, as if in answer to my despair, as we drove past the parkland of Pleys Castle a familiar white car shot out of the ornate gates and my heart jumped for joy as I saw its russet-headed driver. I knew the answer to my problem. My love for Adam Hebburn had taken me beyond the realms of reason, a wild insensate love that is complete obession, that can blithely ignore any impediment (such as a missing wife), and can afford to look no further than today for its promises of bliss.

At my side, Warren cursed, giving the other car room to pass and, unable to bear his caustic comments, I kept silent over the driver's identity. I looked at my watch. It was ten-thirty and I knew that never an early riser, Adam had spent the night at Pleys Castle. I felt bitterly wounded that after our affectionate leave-taking he had been so near and had never called.

No longer listening to Warren's chatter, I told myself sternly that Adam had every right to visit Lady Ester Pleys, who was his sister's friend, and what business was it of mine. Yet the hurt remained and the first thing I asked Dad when I got home was: 'Any phone calls for me?'

In retrospect those days at home were bright with revelations. In truly heroic form, they came in threes, all from very different sources and all recognisably plain warnings of the set-up at Whitton Sands. But my poor guardian angel was working overtime and all for nothing. His protégée, Julie Marsden, blinded by love, had neither wit nor will to read the signs so painstakingly set before her.

The first revelation came innocently enough from the lips of Mrs. Browne. That Rev. Scales had once been vicar of the Abbey Church at Corham.

The second was a front-page picture in a week-old Newcastle paper, as I put a stack of them out on bin-day. There was Penelope Riche's wedding in the Guards Chapel, London. 'The daughter of the late Sir Samuel and Lady Riche of Pasmanton, Northumberland, and sister of Dr. Philip Riche who is in practice in the county ... Among the guests at the wedding was her grandmother, Lady Ester Pleys of Pleys Castle ...'

The third revelation followed swiftly on the heels of the other two. Remembering my promise to Dad about his *Border Badmen*, I took the huge scrapbook up to bed with me. Throughout the years Dad had carefully collected newspaper clips of North-East criminals, some of them he could never use while they lived, unless the law of libel was considerably changed. However, among the yellowed papers I found myself staring into a familiar face.

The face of Strachan, the innkeeper at Whitton Sands and Melanie's stepfather.

Without a doubt it was the same man, although the head was bald, his present suspiciously black hair undoubtedly a toupee. Fascinated I read how years ago he had embezzled money from the Newcastle bank where he worked over a long period. Then by an irony of fate when he was on war service, and had won the Victoria Cross, it all came to light. Subsequently he went to jail. One of the chief character witnesses at the trail was Lady Ester Pleys, for he had been her nephew's batman and had saved his life under fire. There followed the usual paragraph about Hector Pleys, his ill-fated end in Africa on location and his great loss to the British stage and film industry, his international reputation as an actor. There was nothing new. I had read it all before.

On Sunday I went to morning service at the Abbey Church, in the hushed reverence of those who customarily draw their spiritual succour from ancient churches, peaceful and empty and smelling of musty bibles and mould.

Under the pulpit was the Pleys family pew.

Lady Ester sat in it alone. She saw me, smiled, and at the church door, with the service over, we met again, when the vicar shook hands with us all. She seemed gratified by my presence in this somewhat unusual setting, asked after Adam and Marie and did I attend St. Cuthbert's at Corham? When I said no, she said sternly:

'You should, you should. It's very ancient, almost as old as our own Abbey.'

I said, rather lamely, that I had met Rev. Scales and his daughter.

For a moment she looked quite put out, even scared. 'Er, such a nice man. A sweet girl, too,' she said, and scuttled away to the waiting car.

I left the old churchyard thoughtfully. Rev. Scales, Penelope Riche and Strachan. I had received three pieces of information. None of them particularly interesting in themselves—even Strachan's prison sentence was a long time ago. None of them particularly interesting, I thought, except—except that the common denominator of all three was Lady Ester Pleys. I walked faster towards the Cloisters. Perhaps I had been a fool to so readily discount that 'Queen of the Smugglers' theory. Perhaps it was nearer the truth than I had first lightheartedly imagined.

I was sorely tempted to share my speculations with someone. And as Warren and I walked by the river, its paths deep in leaves that afternoon, I had my opportunity. He was very interested in hearing all about my life at Whitton Sands.

But somehow I held my tongue and was even rather guarded in my replies to his innocent questions. Whatever plot was afoot, if it concerned Adam Hebburn, I would unravel it myself, without the help of the entire Northumberland Constabulary.

It was an insane and dangerous decision, but I was still naive enough to believe that love conquers all things, especially devils. Including whatever devilry lurked at Whitton Sands ...

CHAPTER 12

Perhaps that was how they intended it to happen. That my visit home, surrounded by those I loved in the safe familiar tempo of Corham life, should lull me into feeling secure again.

Perhaps they were even frightened. Just a little.

Whatever the intention, it succeeded beyond their wildest dreams. The revelations concerning Rev. Scales, Penelope Riche and Strachan, and their strange connection with Lady Ester Pleys, held no significance for me, no warning. But as Mum recovered I counted the days until my return to Priory House. And, of course, to Adam Hebburn.

Often as I worked by the kitchen window with its distant prospect of hills, wondering sentimentally if Adam missed me, I chuckled over the nonsense of imagining that Whitton Sands was involved in some weird smuggling melodrama, with Adam or the Hermit of Whitton Peel as leader. Like the legend of King Arthur and his knights waiting inside Ninespears Crag, it took on the absurdity of some wild dream remembered in waking hours. The only reality was my love for Adam, as painful and real as toothache. I had to be with him, whatever the conditions. To think that I had objected to being, as I fancifully thought, prisoner in Priory House, Adam's prisoner ...

Had I entertained a moment's fleeting sanity, I might have considered that over a couple of kisses I behaved like a prize idiot. Bad enough that my love for Charlie was composed of virtuous hypocrisy doomed to early disaster had he lived, but straight from that unwholesome self-deceit I had embarked on the sordid recklessness of infatuation for a married man, considerably older than myself, whose wife was meantime conveniently off-stage.

From the sexless cuddle I had expected of marriage with Charlie I had graduated to 'love' as an eternal bedroom scene from an X film, its ending the morning's goodbye between sophisticated people merely consoling each other, with neither recriminations nor consequences of their folly.

When Mum announced that she was quite capable of taking over the household, especially the kitchen, again, I tried not to run to the telephone. Marie seemed glad to hear from me and said Adam would come next morning.

The car arrived, he greeted us cheerfully, politely concerned for my mother's health. But although I watched and listened carefully, I could not detect anything in their behaviour to indicated the familiarity I had suspected on their earlier meeting, or when Adam had found his way to the house unaided by directions from me.

Soon we were driving away, I was waving to Mum telling her: 'Take care.' As we left Corham behind, suddenly shy at Adam's nearness, sure of his awareness of my loving glances. I asked about Marie.

'She's been working very hard all week. And, what's more, she's been slave-driving me too. As you doubtless observe.' He raised stained fingers on the wheel. 'One of her artist friends in the States sent her some great new ink, quite indelible. I don't know yet about it being great, but it's certainly indelible—quite resistant to every known detergent. Anyway, Julie, thanks to your help, Marie reckons there's about one week's work before the book is finished. You've been marvellous, it would have taken us months to compile that index alone ...

One week. What superb irony, I thought, to

have been such a devoted and industrious secretary that I had worked myself right out of Adam Hebburn's world.

As Adam talked, he stared straight ahead, and embarrassed by the memory of the affectionate leave-taking when he deposited me at the Cloisters, I was mortified, sure that his cheerful, casual manner clearly meant a change of heart. *If,* indeed, his heart had been involved at all, his affection the spontaneous reaction of an attractive man unable to resist an easy conquest.

Panic-stricken, I saw him completely aware of my adoration, horrified at getting himself into an emotional entanglement and rushing home to Whitton Sands, appealing to Marie for a speedy completion of her book. Anything, for heaven's sake, to rid himself of my starry-eyed devotion.

Feeling crushed and miserable, I edged as far away from him as possible, hopes of the lovers' meeting I had imagined bleakly retreating as the miles to Priory House diminished. My whole life seemed suddenly composed of instable but glorious day-dreams, and I thought gloomily of the picture that vanity had painted. How having been parted for a few days, he might even say he had missed me.

Ten minutes from the crossroads the route takes a sharp tumble from the Military Road's precision to meander briefly through a pretty glade down by the river. Suddenly Adam slowed down, took a right turn and drove the car into a secluded belt of trees.

He looked round, switched off the engine and kissed me. Taken completely by surprise, there was nothing prim or self-conscious in my response. A moment later he smiled and released me, to sit back regarding me rather narrowly.

'Well, Julie,' he said.

'Well, Adam,' I replied cheerfully, very pleased with myself.

He frowned. 'It isn't "well, Adam" and you known damn fine. I've missed you like hell since you left, counting the hours like a green lovesick boy.'

'I've counted the hours too,' I murmured.

But he shrugged away from me. 'No, no, Julie. This won't do. For one thing I have a wife, officially, anyway.'

'I don't care. Adam darling, if she doesn't love you, then I do.'

'And what exactly does *that* little speech mean?'

'I love you. And I don't care whether the relationship is permanent or not. After all, marriage is a lot of establishment nonsense, probably in fifty years it will be extinct, and good riddance too. Besides, I've been engaged before,' I added carelessly, hoping to sound sophisticated enough not to scare him off, 'and I don't know that I care to be tied again.'

'Tied,' he said roughly, and dragged me by the shoulders so that I faced him. 'You'll be tied to me if I want you to be. And I'll tie you so that you'll damn well never be free again.' He kissed me savagely and it hurt. 'Sorry, Julie, but don't give me your permissive society cant, or those wistful hints about bed, wed or unwed. It just isn't in character with my prim Victorian miss.'

'I am *not* ...'

'Oh yes you are, and make no mistake about it—that's part of your charm.' He wagged an admonishing finger at me. 'So don't try to spoil my illusions. Understand? And don't look so glum. You'll probably get your happy ending some day—if my wife turns up. Alive or dead.'

Alive or dead. And mention of Melanie was a sad grey blight over my unexpected happiness. 'You really think she's still alive?'

'Could be. She could be hiding out in a dozen places, for her own particular reasons. She never lacked friends of her own curious kind.'

'But all this time ...'

He shook his head. 'Not to her. It's happened before.'

'Then surely you should have done something about it?'

'Like what? I'd look pretty stupid when she walked in, demanding to know what all the fuss was about.' He frowned. 'You know, I'm almost certain she wasn't in that plane at all.'

'Adam, why should she play such a horrid trick on you?'

He smiled wryly. 'Because she was that sort of person. You know the kind—who didn't want to be tied.' He stroked my hair. 'Listen, honey, will you? I know it sounds corny, but I'm forty and you're—what? Twenty-four. I probably sound dangerously near the cynical "wife-doesn't-understand me" age. Oh, you'll laugh at all this some day, no doubt, and I hope to heaven you do. But when I'm with you I feel as if this blasted old world is newly born. I felt a hundred years old when I was with Melanie.'

He was silent, gnawing his lip and I said: 'Tell me about her—if it helps.'

'In the first place she wasn't particularly the mate I would have chosen, but I married her to please someone to whom I owed a great debt of gratitude. An insane thing to do, but I was young and fascinated by her and I did fall in love with her. I hoped she felt the same, but she made it clear that all she wanted was the prestige of being wife to a famous painter, especially after the success of "The October Witch". She saw herself sought after by other painters, an international model, and when that didn't happen she was furious, bored to death with Priory House.

'She needed little encouragement to flirt with Philip Riche. That didn't bother me until it became an affaire and Marie was the sufferer. Melanie meant Marie to find out and, of course, she was terribly upset. On the day after, she had the riding accident on Thunder, which probably means she's crippled for the rest of her life.

'I did what was expected of the outraged husband, knocked Philip down in the good old English way and told him never to darken my door again. Of course, I'm aware that he does when I'm away and that Marie has forgiven him. Heaven knows how that will all end,' he added gloomily.

'Anyway, my fury wasn't as jealous husband—there had been too many other men since we married for that. It was because Marie was my sister and I knew that although everyone Melanie encountered adored her, even a little girl like Diane, followed her everywhere, she was one of nature's destroyers ...'

I thought of how she had succeeded with Diane, the lie that sent me to Ninespears Crag, the mischief that bubbled inside the girl.

'... Melanie was willing to put up with me in case I could do another "October Witch". But I never really had any desire to achieve great fame. I don't even think I've got great talent, just two lucky breaks—Hector Pleys, then Melanie. However, Melanie persuaded me to have an exhibition in Newcastle. That convinced me all right. True, I sold a few paintings, but the critics were scathing—said I was cashing in on an old reputation, with nothing new to offer, mediocre. Only a certain youthful talent had not matured. Adam Hebburn had lost the spell. I came home, took the remaining paintings out of the car, carried them into the garden and made a bonfire. Melanie was furious. 'You sold six of them for three hundred guineas. Do you realise what you've done, you damned idiot—you've burned a thousand pounds?'

'She tried to drag them out of the fire,

screaming at me. I watched her and felt nothing. Nothing at all. I knew why I'd never be a great artist. I was dead inside and Melanie had killed me.'

There was silence between us, then he sighed. 'It was all my own fault. Nobody was to blame, not even Melanie. One shouldn't marry to pay off debts of gratitude, that's all.'

It didn't take much fevered deduction to guess that the person to whom Adam Hebburn owed a debt of gratitude was the man who long ago gave him his chance as a portrait painter.

'Not even to Hector Pleys?' I said lightly.

He whistled. 'You're a clever girl, aren't you? And I was so pleased that I had found a connection between Melanie, Hector Pleys and Adam's visit to Pleys Castle I failed to notice there was an edge of mockery in his voice.

'And what was Melanie? His illegitimate daughter?'

Adam's eyebrows raised. 'Right first time.'

Even I was taken aback by the success of that inspired guess. 'How amazing.'

'Not really. Old Hector was something of a sexual athlete.'

'Do you know, the other day you reminded me of him?'

Adam laughed. 'Surely not, Julie honey. I

247

haven't even started on you yet,' he added, with a wicked look.

I blushed. 'Idiot. I meant in looks,' I considered him. 'No—it's gone. It's height and build more than anything. Your face is quite different.'

'To have produced me, Hector would have had to start his amatory career round about thirteen, if that's what you're thinking. Which makes Melanie my half-sister, and only the Pharoahs really weren't shocked by brother-sister marriages. Well, Miss Sharp Eyes, congratulations on a pretty good try.' He tapped his fingers on the steering wheel. 'There is a connection, but not that one ...'

'Tell me.'

Adam frowned. Outside the bright day had vanished and rain battered hard against the roof of the car. 'Symbolic, eh?' he said, and started the engine.

'Please tell me.'

'No. Not until we get home. It's a long story and you might as well hear it in comfort. Besides, this rain's deafening.'

Half an hour later, in the drawing-room of Priory House, Adam handed me a sherry. 'Want something stronger? No? You may need it.'

248

The house was empty, but he hadn't even touched my hand since we came in. 'Marie's in Berwick with Grandpa. I have to collect her later,' he said. 'The old man gets worse every day, madder and wilder. *She* thinks she can sort him out. I don't know what the solution to that problem might be ...'

I wasn't interested. Only at that moment, in Hector Pleys. My impatience must have shown, because he grinned, took a sip of his whisky and said: 'Cheers. Now where were we? Ah yes, my strange resemblance to Hector.' And as he leaned over the settee, smiling at me, I saw it clearly again. 'What was it you said? Height and build, more than anything else.' He looked across, laughing. 'Come on, Miss Sharp Eyes, you're slipping. Surely you know the answer to that one.'

'No, I don't. Should I?'

'Perhaps not. We didn't exactly spread it around. You see, Hector, like many of the other great stars of his time, had his fame partially dependent on epics and the athletic ability to swing from balconies, leap off cliffs, teeter along the parapets of bridges ... But the poor devil had vertigo. He had no head for heights. Where he could tackle anything on the ground, if you lifted him six feet into the air he went to pieces, nauseated, paralysed with fear.'

'But how did you meet him?'

'I'm coming to that. It was when we lived in California and I fancied myself as an artist and was getting nowhere fast, seeking fame and fortune in Hollywood, where Marie knew someone, who knew someone ... Perhaps you've realised I never did have much taste for the rat-race, they call it "lack of ambition", I believe. My folks thought I'd do better in Britain as a farmer, so I came over to stay with Grandpa Hebburn and learn the ropes.

'That summer a scriptwriter friend of Marie's came to visit. He was working on one of the epics they made up here. No, they didn't need artists, but were desperate for extras. I could even commute to location each day, all expenses paid.'

'Wasn't that *Hadrian the Great?* Some of the background shots were Ninespears Crag?'

'Yes. A bit before your time.'

'I saw it on television. It was marvellous.'

Adam bowed. 'Glad you liked it. Anyway, that first glimpse of my ancestral land was never alien to me, as La Jolla, where I was born and raised, was. I reckoned it was because my parents were terribly British that I could never assimilate as the one hundred per cent genuine

American boy. I was always conscious of being grafted on, instead of belonging.'

He walked to the window and stared into the rain. 'I knew the first day I saw Whitton Sands and stood by the tomb of Adam de Hebbyrne that I had come home. Some day when I'm famous, I told myself, I'll settle down here and paint what I want to paint for the rest of my life. But to get back to Hadrian. Remember any of the fight scenes?'

'Scores of them. Especially one of Hadrian trapped by Picts—or was it Scots?—leaping from Ninespears Crag on to a horse's back.'

Adam chuckled. 'That was me. No, not the horse, idiot. I *was* Hadrian in all those action scenes, and a hundred others. The first day I went on set as a humble extra, very proud of my handsome blue toga. During the coffee break someone slapped me on the back and said: 'Hi, Hector.' Later I noticed that walking away from people, they mistook me for him. The producer decided this wouldn't do, I was too tall, too regal, for an extra—no one, but no one, must outshine the Maestro. Somehow it got to Hector's ears. He thought it was a great joke. He sent for me, said: "Got any head for heights, son?" And I was in.

'Hector was interested in everyone. From the

bosomy star to the humblest scene-shifter. For the duration of the film we were just one great happy family, with Hector as king. He remembered names, where he'd met some guy before, even if it was years back. It was all part of his star quality. I suppose he was born a "gentleman" in the old-fashioned sense of the word and he never lost his breeding. Except where women were concerned, and then he was just an alley-cat.

'He not only liked people, he genuinely adored animals. Heaven help anyone found maltreating them on location. Animals in captivity drove him wild—remember the two eagles who attacked Hereward? Well, they were stars in *Sunrise at Avalon*. Afterwards he freed them.'

'I remember noticing a peregrine, just like Hereward in that film.'

'That was his dad. Marvellous actor, he was. Perhaps that's why old Hereward is so humanised. Well, Hector took me back to Hollywood with him, we did a couple of films, then to Rome. While we were there I was always missing, haunting the art galleries and he discovered my real flair was for painting. Two minutes later he was on the telephone to a great friend, who just happened to be one of the best portrait painters in the world ...' and

Adam mentioned a man even I had heard of. 'I studied with him in Rome for a year, then I went back to the States and Hector insisted I paint him as King Arthur. What a chance for an unknown ...

'Soon afterwards he went to Africa on that last ill-fated location. But this time I was to stay at home and paint. I was too valuable. I might get my hands damaged.' Adam smiled. 'It was typical of Hector. He could get a stand-in with a head for heights and a bit of clever camera-work would see him through, but an artist— oh no, they were different. To be cossetted, cherished.

'He was a great man. A legend in his own time. Playing King Arthur all those years, on stage and screen, playing characters always larger-than-life, perhaps the old ghosts crept into him. Who knows? You were too young to remember World War II but Hector was deco-rated twice, you know. He was no star-playing soldier to impress the troops either, loving the uniform and the pips, but keeping well away from the action. He was wounded at Alamein, he was with the first D-day landings in Europe. Do such men ever die?'

It wasn't really a question, because he con-tinued: 'Sorry I get carried away when I talk about him.'

'Where did Melanie fit into all this?'

'As you may know, despite three wives and countless mistresses over the years, all Hector Pleys, great virile star, sex symbol, ever produced were two illegitimate daughters. Melanie to his Guinivere in *King Arthur*. Ironically, she was the only woman he ever cared about and the only woman who, free to marry him, refused to do so.'

I remembered stories about the completely dedicated actress who shunned the limelight and how shocked everyone was when she died of leukaemia.

'Hector never got over her death and Melanie was adopted by Strachan and his wife, here at Whitton Sands. Hector thought the world of Strachan, who had been his batman and saved his life during the war.'

'I know. I was reading about it in some newspaper clippings of Dad's—he's writing a book.'

Adam nodded absently.

'You said two daughters. What happened to the other one?'

'I'm coming to that. Her mother was a waitress at the hotel where Hector stayed when he was acting in a Shakespeare season at the

Theatre Royal in Newcastle.' From behind the settee he took a folder, opened it.

'Take a look at this.' And he handed over a glossy reproduction of the portrait of Hector as King Arthur. 'Hasn't something else quite remarkable struck you about that picture? I thought you might have noticed it in the original at Pleys Castle?'

I stared, seeing nothing.

'His face. Those eyes,' said Adam, 'those quite remarkable eyes, Julie. Their colour.' The eyes in the painting looked back at me, sad, deep blue and inescapable, as Adam continued: 'Go on, don't be afraid. Remember I once said that your eyes belonged in a flower-garden, not in a human face?'

I stared at him. 'Yes, Julie. That's your answer. You're the other daughter.'

I sat down, suddenly weak at the knees, seeing the pattern of the jigsaw slowly take shape. So many small things, apparently insignificant. Right at the beginning my resemblance to Melanie and the fright I had given Adam at first meeting. And how very soon afterwards the Marsdens had told me I was adopted ...

'Of course,' said Adam, helping himself to another drink, 'until I mistook you for Melanie that night in the mist on the road out there he never suspected your existence.'

'How could he suspect my existence? Adam, he's been dead for fifteen years.'

Adam smiled. 'By no means, Julie. He's very much alive and eager to meet you.'

'But where does he live?'

'Very near you. Here in Whitton Peel.'

My hand flew to my throat. 'Not—the Hermit,' I whispered, trying to keep the horror out of my voice.

'Good Heavens, no. Our Hermit was living there long before Hector found it also a convenient place to retire from the world.' As I sighed with relief, Adam looked at his watch. 'You're to go over and see him immediately after lunch. Precisely two hours from now ...'

CHAPTER 13

I asked the inevitable question.

'Oh, yes, your mother is alive—she had you adopted. Don't look like that, Julie, had she been older it might have been different. You see, she was only seventeen when you were born. Presumably Hector didn't stop to ask her age first.' Adam smiled. 'Sorry, that was tactless. Anyway, she was an orphan, raised by a great-aunt who promptly threw her out. Her only relative was an older cousin, whom she'd met perhaps twice. This cousin and her husband were childless ...'

'The Marsdens?' I remembered my strong resemblance to Mum which had puzzled me when I knew I was adopted. Remembered, too, that only cousin in Canada and a certain reluctance to discuss her which now took on a new significance.

Adam nodded. 'They told me this side of the story when I tracked you down to Corham.'

'But didn't they know Hector Pleys was

my father?'

'Frankly, I gather they didn't believe a word of the girl's story. The waitress and the great star. Poor Jean could hardly prove it, she was one girl among a dozen who crawled into Hector's bed whenever he was on tour.

'The Marsdens told me the day she walked into the house was like a miracle. They decided right away whoever was the father they were going to have you when you were born and they persuaded Jean to lie low and say nothing about it. Not very difficult in an isolated house on the moors. Anyway, Jean had no objections—she was grateful and happy with the Marsdens' adoption arrangements. She wanted nothing from Hector Pleys. She didn't want any scandal, just that the baby should have a good home. I gather she was pretty but a shy, uncommunicative girl, who had landed in this mess by her inexperience—hadn't even had a boy friend before.'

'Well, when you were six months old, she got the chance of going to Canada as children's nurse to a local family who had emigrated. A few years later she married there and has children of her own.'

'Why on earth didn't Mum and Dad tell me all this when they told me I was adopted?'

'Because Hector wouldn't agree. This was to be his show, Julie. He wanted to have you at Whitton Sands, get to know you. Then in some great dramatic moment he was to tell you himself. This was to be his greatest role. Thank heaven I persuaded him out of that one. It seemed to me a piece of news better broken delicately.'

'You all took your time getting round to it, I must say. I guessed something was going on here and fondly imagined any number of sinister computations, smuggling included.'

'Sorry, Julie. but that's the way the Maestro wanted it. And as well as liking his own way, he has some very neurotic fears. Like being found still alive—a great hoax. He has a lot to lose, a comfortable way of life at Whitton Sands—and don't tell me there isn't something faintly ridiculous in being resurrected after you're dead for fifteen years.'

'Think of *that* in the hands of the newspapers and you'll feel more sympathy for old Hector. There was something else, too. All his acting career had been haunted by blackmailers of one kind or another. 'She doesn't know me, I mean nothing to her—what if she sees this as a great chance of blackmail?' So—he wanted you established at Priory House with regular progress reports on your character.'

'I still don't get it. It all seems unnecessarily complicated when a simple explanation from Mum and Dad would have been enough for me.'

Adam laughed. 'Simplicity never appealed to Hector. He adores secrecy—perhaps it's a normal reaction from someone who's always under the public eye.' He paused. 'I'd better warn you that no one who has lived his kind of life, emerges at the end of it as normal as the rest of us ...'

'You're not breaking it to me gently that my father is some kind of a nut, are you?'

'Of course not. Just a little eccentric. And he likes his own way. Perhaps if he had inherited Pleys it would have been different. However, there wasn't a hope of that—it goes to a cousin with five sons. Hector liked to imagine himself as the great feudal lord. It was a part he could play to perfection. At least he had money to buy Whitton Sands and the silence of people he could trust. Strachan and Melanie lived in this house. Long before the funeral at Pleys Castle he had it all worked out.'

'Then who is buried in the vault there?'

'One of his African extras who got mauled by a crocodile in a rapids-shooting scene.

Hector loved the idea of this unknown lad being buried with all that pomp at Pleys. 'If ever there's a holocaust and the graves are opened, someone's in for a terrible shock when they discover that Hector Pleys was black.'

'Who arranged all the details?'

'I did. With Lady Ester's connivance, of course. I thought I was going to the airport to escort his body home. I was so upset I could hardly think straight. Then in the car-park there was this African chief, all fuzzy grey hair, feathers and white draperies, sitting in the back of a Rolls. I'd been told he was waiting for me. 'You Adam Hebburn, mister?' he said. 'We talk private. In here. I bring message.' As the chauffeur drove off past all the reporters and crowds waiting to pay their last respects, he dug me in the ribs and said 'Well Adam, how are you? You old son-of-a-gun? Sorry you won't be able to grow fat on my insurance for a while yet.'

Adam smiled. 'I was never so delighted to see anybody in my life. It was like those dreams you get when someone you love dies. Miraculously they're alive again, it's all been a terrible nightmare.' For a moment he looked so sad. I wondered how often he had that one about Melanie. 'Between the airport and Pleys we hatched the final details of the plot. I was to claim the insurance and Hector's estate as sole beneficiary. Whitton Sands was on its last legs and Strachan had been instructed to buy out the remaining three fishing families for a substantial sum and replace them with servants from Pleys who could be trusted.

'The man you call the Hermit, Jim Elliott, already lived in Whitton Peel. He was happy to share it with Hector, whom he had known back in the Army days. Hector had a fellow feeling for Elliott's disfigurement in that burning tank during the desert campaign. He could understand the man's motive for retirement, knowing that crippled, partly paralysed, he would never again be looked on without pity. Especially by women. Women the world over who adored him.

' "Death, my dear boy, is preferable to obscurity. And pity disgusts me. It's too tiresome,' he said, 'and I can't bear being tiresome.' When I argued he said: 'My dear Adam, I've seen situations like this before. Oh, there would be plenty of parts coming my way—at first. Because producers would be sorry—must do something for poor old Hector. But later on? What then? I don't want favours, I've too much pride, always had. Help me, old son. Remember when the great fall they fall a lot further than common mortals ever dream of." So I helped him set up the stage at Whitton Sands.'

'Stage was the right word,' I said, remembering Rev. Scales, who had been vicar at Corham until drink drove him; Philip Riche who was related to Hector; Strachan who had been his batman. 'A doctor to cure, a parson to bury and a devoted servant. No wonder I thought Whitton Sands was phoney, a stage set for a great spectacular that was never made. At least you aren't all smugglers, as I thought at first. The only part that didn't fit was Lady Ester—I simply couldn't imagine her up to something discreditable. And I suppose Mrs. Miles' wardrobe mistress days were with Hector?'

'Right,' said Adam. 'She was always longing to talk about them. The weakest link in the chain. She stayed with us out of devotion, but it must have seemed very odd that a noted historian's widow needed to do housework around the village.' He looked at his watch. 'Well, that's the story, Julie. Now I'll have to go. Make your own way over, will you, when it's time. You know the way. Just open the door and walk in—he'll be waiting for you.'

'Aren't you coming with me? I think I need your moral support.'

Adam smiled thinly. 'Oh no. He'd be embarrassed by my presence on this occasion. Besides, I have to collect Marie from Grandpa's and see my falconer friend to discuss Hereward's matrimonial prospects. He's hand-reared a young female and thinks she'd be the perfect mate for him.'

At the door he looked back, uncomfortably, I thought afterwards, sure that his too hearty: 'Well, good luck. See you,' wasn't really what he wanted to say, nor was his abrupt departure the only reason I felt so bereft.

There was something wrong. But what? Could it be *only* because he hadn't kissed me? And as I went upstairs and sat at the dressing-table and made up my face in suitable manner for a daughter meeting her famous long-lost father for the first time, there was a weight like lead at my heart.

It was all wrong. With so many suspicions cleared away, so many threads tied, there should have been a strengthening of the bond between Adam and me. I tried to see him through dispassionate eyes. This strange man whom I'd met so little time ago. The Horseman who emerged like a legend come to life, from the mists on Ninespears Crag, a ghostly reincarnation from another age, the Crusader whose

264

tomb I had found, the shock of loving a man who had been dead for eight hundred years ...

Yet, like some fantastic fairy-tale, it had all come true, far beyond anything even my imagination could have dreamed up. Incredible, this man of flesh and blood was mine. Today, tomorrow—hadn't he assured me of a 'happy ending' once Melanie reappeared? Alive or dead, as he grimly put it. Either out of the sea, where no one seemed able to prove she had met her death, or alive from London, Paris, or God knows where, caring for nobody, least of all her husband. 'The October Witch', with a vengeance ...

In view of what I now knew about Melanie, perhaps I was being too humble, too in awe of Adam Hebburn's love. Perhaps the reason he loved me was that I was so different and ordinary, a complete contrast except in looks, to Melanie. It was all so simple. Adam had kissed me and I had fallen in love with him. A few days' parting in which to miss each other and a lovers' meeting. A perfect vignette of Victorian romance. Yet my very skin crept with prickles of misgiving, for something deep inside me said: 'It had all been *too* simple.

A famous father discovered in a tide of romance. Adam's love. There had to be a flaw somewhere, something to spoil that happy ending Adam had promised me. For instance, had he told me he loved me in as many words? I couldn't remember. And what if Melanie didn't turn up? The prospect of waiting didn't bother me, shrouded in all the certainty of a day's love. But as days turned into months and years, what then? Wouldn't patience and content turn a little sour, love wilt a little at the edges?

I went downstairs again, feeling treacherous and disloyal. Poor Adam, was it *his* fault that his wife had disappeared, cruelly enjoying his discomfort? Here I was with all my dreams come true, being thoroughly selfish, full of gloomy forebodings just because my pride was hurt that Adam hadn't kissed me goodbye. Well, I could soon remedy that I'd tell him and he'd laugh, assure me it was all nerves. And, of course, he loved me. That was all I needed to satisfy my dread feeling that there were still a thousand things unsaid between us, a thousand shadows ...

There was no reply to my knock at the study door. The room was empty.

'Adam, Adam,' I called upstairs. The house was empty too, although I hadn't heard him leave but the car was gone from the drive.

'Adam,' I kept on calling. The house seemed

very still. Silent and ominous, as if the very walls listened ... And as I stood nervously in the dark panelled hall I remembered that these walls had not always been so tranquil, they had known treachery and sudden bloody death. Perhaps the imprints of those terrible days still hung there, ghosts without hope of appeasement.

I ran into the kitchen. 'Adam, where are you?' I opened the back door. And all at once I remembered. Of course, he would be with Starlight. Should I follow him? And pride said, No, you've made fool enough of yourself for one day ...

Deciding to be sensible, I went back to the study where it was perfectly obvious neither Adam nor Marie knew the meaning of tidiness. From the neat well-ordered room I had kept, with an efficient new filing system hidden away in the cupboard, chaos had taken over. I set to work, seeing myself through the years looking after Adam, sorting socks, sewing buttons on shirts. The idea made him suddenly very human, and ours an ordinary undramatic marriage despite its hectic prelude.

There was therapy in tidying, I hoped, emptying the waste-paper basket and gathering the box files which were strewn on every available chair. I would be sure of Adam, I would be joyful and excited—and not so idiotically suspicious of everything and everybody. But as I worked, instead of joy and excitement, I felt further cast out from him than any mere absence of an affectionate leave-taking could explain. As time passed, there was a distinct chill of apprehension growing in the region of my heart. Suddenly I wished I had stayed at home in Corham and had never heard of Hebburns or Hector Pleys. I longed for Mum and Dad, and even Warren, just a little, whose behaviour was at least predictable and whose absence stirred kindlier thoughts in me than his presence ever did.

When at last I walked through Melanie's garden on my way to Whitton Peel, mellow sunlight shone through the trees, like great spotlights on a superb stage. An orchestra of melancholy sparrows tuned up and seagulls with great mocking cries began the overture ...

It was the perfect setting for a romantic meeting and I defied Hector Pleys himself to have thought up a more extravagant set. I wondered how he would greet me. Possibly by asking after the Marsdens, who must have visited him that day at Priory House, when I saw them leave and thought they were smugglers too. Now it had all been so simply explained.

Or had it? Letting myself into Whitton Peel, as Adam had instructed, I found before me a long stone corridor ending in an old oak door. I rapped on it, waited, hoping I wouldn't be met by the Hermit and have to hide my horror and smile politely into that poor broken, terrible face.

No one came and I opened the door. I blinked at the scene, for somehow I had slipped back in time and strolled right into the thirteenth century. A great stone hall, an enormous round table. Tattered battle flags hanging from the rafters. And watching me, a crowd of menacing knights, larger than life, their maces raised. I blinked again, saw that knights were only suits of armour, their visors down, their swords and weapons harmless ...

Someone had made excellent and effective use of the props from *Sunrise at Avalon*. And there at the table, in a crowned and canopied chair, sat King Arthur himself. In a purple velvet robe, at his right hand on the table, a horn lay, waiting. Behind his chair a hooded grey figure hovered, the Hermit ... I looked away quickly.

'Please sit down, Julie. Yes, yes, where you are. That will do splendidly.' It was too dark for me to see him clearly, but the black curly hair was still recognisably Hector Pleys'. 'How nice to see you, my dear.' He cleared his throat, the action nervous but unnecessary, for the voice millions had loved was shades too loud for an audience of one, seated twelve feet away. His voice penetrated, reverberated in every corner of the hall, but its magic had gone. It sounded cracked, awful, like a great bell rusted with disuse and reminded me of a local opera singer, long past the age of decent retirement who tried out a few songs at a charity concert in Corham, to please some adoring relatives and a few elderly fans.

'Forgive me for not rising, my dear. Are you quite comfortable?' He would make no move to show his crippled state. I could tell Adam that even for his daughter Hector Pleys hadn't lost his vanity.

'I am so glad Adam discovered you, Julie. I hope we're going to be friends. This meeting doesn't embarrass you? Good.' He laughed silently. 'I wouldn't wish you to be distressed. Now that you're staying in Whitton Sands perhaps we can have many little meetings. I would greatly appreciate your company, my dear. I'm a lonely old man, you know.' He paused, perhaps waiting for me to contradict him. Then he sighed. 'I'm a very sick old man, too. Very sick, Julie. My heart, you know. The merest exertion ...' He made a fluttering gesture and shook his head significantly.

I listened, waiting to feel stricken, to feel pity and anguish for him. Waiting to feel *some* emotion for this strange man who was my real father. But I felt nothing. Nothing. Not pity, not even liking for the shadowy figure in the chair opposite. I would have felt more emotion —and, indeed, often have—for a crippled street singer, a blind beggar.

As I sat bolt upright in the hard chair, smiling politely, I was like a spectator at an amateur play one wants to like very much—because the leading actor is a good kind friend, a close relative, but all the time one is conscious of the atrocious acting, the dreadful set.

My eyes were growing used to the dimly lit hall and I could see him clearly. His face, half-turned from me, had the same mask-like beauty I remembered from his films. A curved mouth moving in a serene, faintly smiling expression. His hands were still young too. Young and rather dirty, and as I somehow lost the thread of a little monologue on his health, which turned into a larger monologue on his distant days of fame, I became aware of a strong smell of carbolic about the place. Uncharitably I wondered whether there was much washing done at Whitton Peel, or whether Hector Pleys retired into King Arthur, in a truly medieval identification, *sans* baths and all ...

As he talked, I was conscious of the Hermit, just a pace behind him, unmoving except for a gloved hand that occasionally drew the hood closer over his face. I burned with shame, remembering how I had yelled in terror at our first encounter. Adam had said Hector would see me alone. I wished I had been spared this embarrassing meeting.

But before I had a chance to throw in more than a dozen words, or to tell him how much I had enjoyed his films (which was true), he was indicating that the interview was at an end. 'You must come again, my dear—quite often. If our meetings are necessarily brief, well, my heart—you understand. Just a few minutes every day, that is all the good Dr. Riche allows for visitors. You may leave us now. Please come again tomorrow.'

He inclined his head in regal dismissal and I made my exit rather too eagerly, with good-byes and sympathetic murmurings about his health, too indecently hurried for conviction. Leaving the hall with its weird furnishings and weirder occupants, I realised that despite his magnificent looks, that amazing appearance of indestructible youth, whatever charm and magnetism he had once possessed were gone. At least he had chosen retirement wisely, with the legend of Hector Pleys unshattered.

I had expected someone quite different. Not just a sick, tired old man, his only interest in this new-found daughter, I suspected, as potential new audience. Quite oblivious to me as a person, he hadn't wanted to know what made me 'tick', completely absorbed by the stories of his own far-off days of grandeur, whining a little about their passing, greatly obsessed with his ill-health. Perhaps astonished to find that Hector Pleys was not, in fact, immortal. Remembering the stumbling voice, the hesitations, I thought of him at a loss to face an audience without a script to follow and plentiful cues from the waiting cast ...

I returned to Priory House through the bright autumn afternoon, with the sun still warm on my face. I was bitterly depressed. What should have been one of the most dramatic moments in my life had somehow managed to fizzle out like a damp squib. I wished Adam would come home, wished I had someone to talk to. The empty house appalled and frightened me, weighing me down with its silence.

And what on earth would I tell Adam when he arrived? Adam, who adored Hector. I imagined him dashing in with Marie, both of them eager and excited, dying to know what I'd thought of my marvellous father. Both of them still seeing Hector Pleys as the great man, the legend. A little in awe of him, with eyes that had never deviated once from hero-worship to see the sad reality and be thankful that sometimes it is kinder for a great actor to die young ...

If there was nobody to talk to, at least there was still plenty of work in the study. I set to work gathering papers into filing order, storing them in the appropriate boxes, with a strong feeling of righteousness. I might not be clever and talented like the Hebburns, but at least I was orderly, neat and reliable. As I worked, I composed and rejected a dozen speeches about Hector. Never a good actress, my disappointment was going to be difficult to conceal. Could I take refuge in such ambiguities as 'fascinating', 'interesting', 'intriguing'—relying on the Hebburns' enormous enthusiasm to receive such words as compliments, my disillusion unobserved.

Disillusion. Perhaps the first shock was

everything. I tried to see myself feeling tenderness for this old man, so divorced from King Arthur or any of the epic characters he had once portrayed. My own father, Hector Pleys ... But it was no use. My own father would always be Dick Marsden, Dad—with his books, his pipes and our long walks together by the river at Corham. Hector Pleys could never take his place.

I knew it was unkind, unreasonable. Hector and I had both been at a disadvantage and the Hermit's presence had put me off, certain he must have told Hector how I had run off, screaming, at his approach. His stilted manner had been guilt and natural embarrassment for the insignificant waitress he couldn't remember and the one lovers' night in thousands that had produced this girl, who looked at him with his own eyes. A daughter, but a complete stranger ...

Only an hour had passed since that ten-minute interview at Whitton Peel. Adam and Marie would not be back before early evening. Suddenly exhausted, drained, I thought of the empty waiting hours, wishing it were nine instead of four, so that I could take a bath and retire to my room without politely waiting for the Hebburns' return.

Closing the last paper into the file, I dusted the desk and decided to take the bath anyway, then I would write some long-overdue letters, including one to my friend Lucy, in Paris at a conference with her scientist husband. If only she were at home, how I would relish her reaction to this new secret ...

Gathering the large pile of box files in my arms, I marched determinedly towards the open cupboard. But the determined march was my undoing. Vision screened by boxes, I failed to notice the flex of a standard lamp across my path. I tripped and with my unsteady load went hurtling into the open cupboard, papers spewing out in all directions.

Grabbing at anything to stop my headlong tumble, my hand touched a hidden lever on the inside wall. I was jolted to a standstill, but, incredibly, the shelves kept on moving. There was a door at the back of the cupboard.

Fascinated, I thought I had stumbled on a secret passage. Long-forgotten tales of secret rooms and hidden treasure from ancient school stories came rushing into my mind. It was all magnificently Cromwellian, a passage which had lain undisturbed since the last smugglers were hanged at Berwick.

Expecting cobwebs and dust, I wedged one

foot into the door, groping in my pocket for my cigarette lighter. But I didn't need it. There on the stone wall inside the passage was a modern plastic light switch. The passage was very well used and far from secret, lit at regular intervals by a cable carrying light bulbs. Modern hands had plastered the walls and whitewashed them too. It was all beautifully clean, as antiseptic and unromantic as a hospital corridor.

With less fear than I approached Whitton Peel for the first time, I followed the tunnel which curved steeply upwards, around to the left. Obviously at some distant date this had been a smugglers' route, its width perfect for the frenzied rolling of casks of brandy and rum. Earlier, it must have formed part of cellars in the medieval Whitton Castle which had been replaced by Priory House ... And it suddenly occurred to me to wonder who had taken the trouble to modernise it to the extent of electricity cables, and for what purpose?

The tunnel ceased abruptly, the ceiling was higher, and I stood in a small cavern, with several other dark passages leading in other directions. I paused hesitating, but straight in front was a very twentieth-century door. Then I was plunged into darkness as the light, controlled by a time-switch went out. In sudden panic I stumbled towards the door I had seen, flicked on my lighter, and there was a very ordinary door-knob, which I turned slowly, expecting it to be locked.

It opened and I almost jumped out of my skin. In front of me a knight in full armour, mace raised ready to strike.

For a dizzy moment I thought of Ninespears Crag, the legend of King Arthur and his knights, waiting. Then I laughed. I knew where I was. The tunnel had sloped upwards and to the left. I was in Whitton Peel again and although my view was partially obscured, it was the same great stone hall where an hour previously I had met Hector Pleys.

There were the suits of armour, the hunting horn on the table, the tattered flags. The carbolic smell hiding dust and decay ...

I heard voices. Craning my head I saw two men. One was the Hermit, his face hidden. The other man had his back to me. A back my senses had recognised even in an old film on television. And my pulse still raced.

He laughed. 'I think we can congratulate ourselves. We succeeded very well indeed. Certainly had Miss Sharp Eyes fooled. Life's full of surprises—when I helped you kill off

Hector, I never expected having to resurrect
him for a farewell tour ...'

The voice belonged to Adam Hebburn.

CHAPTER 14

'Yes, we've certainly got Miss Sharp Eyes
fooled.' Adam was looking down at the purple
velvet robe draped over the canopied chair
beside it a dark curly wig lay limply on the
table, attached to something pink and grue
somely deflated. A mask—all that remained o
Hector Pleys.

'I'm a better actor than you give me credi
for,' said Adam proudly. 'And that concealed
microphone was an inspiration.'

The Hermit's shoulders shook. He wa
laughing.

'What do you mean,' demanded Adam, '
looked like a ventriloquists's dummy?' Sudden
ly serious, he said: 'How should I know where
we go from here? I'm clear out of ideas, and
you know damned well I never cared for thi
one. I only hope that resurrecting poor old Hec
tor doesn't prove to be our greatest mistake
I think we should have left him to rest in peace
Quite, quite dead.'

The Hermit's back was still towards me, his reply muffled by the hood. 'Oh God,' Adam laughed bitterly, *'you're* a bit late with the sentiment ... Sorry, sorry—the whole situation makes me nervous, I guess. Too many things can go wrong.' As he spoke he tapped his fingers against the dead man's mask on the table, hands still grimy from indelible ink. Small wonder I had thought Hector Pleys had young hands ... Adam Hebburn's hands.

The Hermit murmured something: 'How—would feel—horror?'

Adam frowned. 'Look, I'm not blaming you or anything. I just don't like the set-up. Personally I have too much to lose this time. You know I've always co-operated in the past, but pure vanity is something I don't understand. I guess because I never had much to be vain about anyway ...'

Was that why he had killed Hector, because he was eaten up with envy? Had he hated him all those years, despised him for his success with women: 'I never had his success,' he said to me—unable even to keep Melanie loving him? Was that the reason men committed murder? Or was it something else, greed, money? And was the Hermit twisted, warped as himself, to be accomplice to murder a helpless crippled man?

'She loves me, you know,' said Adam, and I realised he was talking about me. 'You're completely forgetting that, aren't you. I think if we told her the truth we could rely on her silence. All girls aren't on the make, you know. And she's nothing like Melanie. She'll do anything I ask her ... In fact,' he said casually, 'I expect I'll marry her—with your approval, of course,' he added mockingly.

So the wheel had turned full circle. But oh the price was greater than ever I could pay. And his words 'marry her, marry her ...' seemed to fill that great stone hall like the final poison to my dying love for him. It wasn't such all-consuming madness, after all, I thought with regret. In the face of murder it wilted and was gone ...

The Hermit whispered. 'No—last appearance—dead.'

'I don't fear the dead, it's the living I'm scared for, right now. But when we agreed to kill off Hector, I'm warning you, this bringing him back to life for a farewell performance is a risky business.'

The Hermit's croaking strangled words were unintelligible. But he seemed to be pleading. It was imperative that I hear what he was saying, that I hear something, some small word, oh God, to vindicate Adam Hebburn, whom I had loved, as my father's murderer.

I took a step forward and that was my undoing. My arm touched the mace in the knight's hand and it fell noisily to the ground.

Both men turned, saw me. Adam rushed forward, surprised, angry. 'Julie, what the devil are you doing snooping about here? Get out—this is no place for you. Get out ...'

'Don't come near me,' I said. 'You—murderers. I'm not scared. You killed my father and you won't get away with it. I'll make sure you don't.'

Adam put his hand on my arm. 'Julie, honey. Listen—you *must* listen ...' He was so close and I was shocked that the old magic still worked. I saw his eyes smiling, anxious, his lips that I had kissed moving towards me. 'Julie ...'

Over his shoulder I watched the Hermit approaching, slowly, leaning on his stick. What I had seen that day in the garden was nothing to the horror before me now. A man or what was left of one, for in that hood was no nylon-stockinged mask this time.

It was the face of a corpse. Only shreds of skin remained on bone, patched here and there, with red and white and dark cavity. Two great empty hollows with the faint glitter of eyes in their depths, a lipless mouth against huge teeth. And the hand holding the stick, a mere fragment of bone ...

How could any human being look like that and live—a monstrous skeleton, a decaying corpse? Horror, terror, disgust, were too much. I screamed.

'Julie,' said Adam, 'it isn't what you think ...' Over his shoulder he said to the Hermit, 'For God's sake, let me tell her ...'

But I was beyond hearing. I had to get away, out of this nightmare back into a world I could recognise, full of ordinary people, *real* people. But Adam held me fast. 'Let me go.' And struggling to free myself, I saw the fallen mace. A weapon to defend myself—if only I could reach it.

'Damn you,' said Adam, suddenly releasing me. 'Then stop behaving like a little fool. If only you'll stop howling—and *listen*—we'll explain it all. It isn't what you think ...'

I dived down, picked up the mace. 'Julie, you wouldn't hit me with that. Julie,' he said softly, 'Come on, hand it over. It's a nasty weapon. It could kill someone. Julie ...'

'Stay away from me. Both of you.'

Adam came a step closer. 'Julie, hand it over.

There's a good girl. Then we'll talk. Come on.'
His voice was growing impatient, he snapped
his fingers—and the gesture rang a bell.

The Horseman of Ninespears Crag, the night
we met with Mini in the ditch. He righted the
car and wordlessly, in this same commanding
gesture, demanded the keys to start her. The
memory didn't belong in this nightmare of intrigue and murder but to an enchanted world
where I could still laugh and dream and forget
that, round the corner, the piper still waited
to be paid.

As he snapped his fingers again, I opened my
eyes wide. Like someone coming out of a hyp-
notic trance. Now I was seeing him for the first
time. Now I was back at the beginning. I was
myself again. Julie Marsden, matter-of-fact, sensible, ordinary girl. And with that snap of the
fingers he had released me from the enchanter's
spell ...

'Come on, Julie, there's a dear.' Impatiently,
he grabbed for the mace, but not quite in time.
I sprang back and brought it down with all
the force I could muster against his head. He
ducked, but wasn't quick enough and his eyes
were still open, still full of surprise and
reproach as he fell. He didn't cry out, he just
gave a small sigh and lay motionless. While

blood, like some monstrous crimson rose, grew around my feet.

In one bound, it seemed, I reached the door behind the suit of armour. The Hermit let out a strangled cry, a word that sounded like: 'Wait.'

For a moment, as the door closed behind me, I leaned weakly against it, hoping I wasn't going to faint for the first time in my life. My legs were like lead. I felt sick, dreadful, ill and fit to die. And contaminated.

I had murdered Adam Hebburn. Even in self-defence, as long as I lived my conscience would never rest again. Better to be dead ...

Then the light went on, activated automatically by the closing of the door and I saw that instead of one tunnel leading back to Priory House, four other dark openings sprouted like the fingers of nightmare's hands. Certain I had come by the furthest right, I ran sobbing down it. At any moment now I would see the door leading back into the study.

After a while, breathless, I stopped. Was it only panic made the tunnel seem endless, and considerably steeper downhill than the way I had climbed before? Then quite suddenly the light went out again. And in the darkness I heard another sound, the echo of halting steps, the tap of a stick.

Behind me, and not far away, the Hermit ...

I was chilled to the heart with fear. The boom I heard wasn't my own heart and I wasted precious seconds to stand still, to listen. Growing louder, rhythmic and eternal, the sound of wave striking rock. And very near at hand. The sea.

I hesitated. I had a choice. To retrace my steps and face the Hermit. Perhaps in a straight fight I could knock him down. Because I was young and strong and had right on my side. Although in real life, I suspected the good ones were often killed off and the bad ones lived to fight another day ... I ran forward. Yes, I'd take any chance with that brutal merciless sea, rather than the human evil behind me.

And the seconds I had wasted to reconsider had been invaluable. Already my eyes were growing accustomed to the gloom and as I ran there was an increasing glow of light.

The tunnel had widened and lightened. The ceiling was higher. I stopped running. I was in an enormous cave. At any other time I would have admired its strange beauty, the green fronds of reflected light dancing above my head. There was a strong smell of the sea, and through a tiny patch of broken rock far above my head I heard seagulls, chuckling against a still bright sky.

I could escape ... But the walls of the cave were perpendicular, smooth green as glass. The path in front of me dipped sharply, twisting, and was blocked completely by fallen boulders from some ancient landslide. A moment later my feet splashed water as I looked up, quite helpless to reach the spot where daylight seeped through. I touched the wall, drew away my hand sharply. It was cold, wet and slimy. Impossible to find a foothold on such a surface.

There was also enough daylight to show an ominous green line all round the cave, extending well above my head. Small wonder the path had dipped so sharply. I was now well below sea-level. At high tide this great cavern would be flooded by the sea.

And was it only fancy that above my head the patch of blue already grew dimmer? I thrust my fist in my mouth, wanting to scream, to go to pieces—anything rather than stand with the first waves licking at my feet and contemplate a slow and lingering death.

I tried to take a grip on myself, panic would be fatal. And calmly, like someone waiting for a bus, I looked at my watch. It was almost four o'clock. And when, oh God, was high tide? Was it only fear and imagination that made the roar of the sea seem louder now?

And then I saw it. I narrowed my eyes afraid to hope. Something I had dismissed at first glance as a crack in the rock extending along the length of the high smooth wall to my right. I saw with delight it was a ledge, a wonderful miraculous, life-saving ledge. And by running back to the cave's entrance, I could reach it. But quicker to climb from here ...

I began. Feet and hands slithered back in wet seaweed. Making little progress, I stopped for breath, listened ... Close at hand I heard another sound.

Someone else was breathing ...

I was too late. Raising my head, I saw the Hermit was already on the ledge, making his way slowly along in my direction. I should have realised he would know the terrain and now he had the advantage of being able to wait patiently and cut off my one line of retreat from the rising tide.

He would wait, knock my hands off the edge with his stick, or with his feet. Even a frail old man could manage that.

But I wasn't beaten yet. I still had a chance, if he didn't know I was here. Away to my right, where the shadows were deeper. Darkness would protect me. There might even be an overhanging rock to hide under ...

As I progressed, slowly, silently, I heard myself whisper: 'Dear God, deliver me from evil ...' I felt so small and insignificant, and sorry too that I hadn't put all those hours of sightseeing in ancient churches to better use, with a prayer or two, an insurance on eternity. I thought of God, imposed upon, long-suffering, absorbed by more important business than pleas for help from a girl who never darkened His doors, except to admire their architecture ...

I hadn't moved more than six feet when I realised darkness was my enemy. There were fewer footholds. My left foot slithered away, then my hand. Slowly I began to slide, to fall, then to roll. I was never sure afterwards whether the scream I heard was real or only inside my head.

Then the breath was jerked out of my body and I lay with bruised knees and my right wrist doubled up under me. A small ledge had broken my fall. I looked upwards. Six feet of smooth rock wall covered in green wet slime. And even as I moved and felt the searing burn of agony in my wrist, I knew that this was one wall I would never climb, even with two good arms.

The ledge was two feet wide. Nothing but a miracle—or that prayer—had stopped me hurtling into the rock-pool below. It was quite a small pool and there was enough light for it to be surprisingly still and mirror-like.

I could see my face reflected, distorted, white and still. My eyes frightened, wide open, looked green in the reflected light. My hair long and dark red, a great mass moving back and fro with the current. My own face, but hideously changed. As if in some monstrous crystal ball of horror, this would be me when I was dead and drowned ...

My eyes were getting used to the dim light. Red hair, green eyes. Some unrecognisable garment, blackened, shredded by the sea, glimpses of body where patches of flesh gleamed white and an arm trailed, the hand moving.

But the fingers were all gone ...

And as the great green sea came rushing eagerly in, I saw this was no reflection in a rock-pool. I sat back in horror and knew I was looking on the face of Melanie.

Even as realisation came, I knew by the boom of the sea and the first wave soaking me to the thighs that I was doomed. The beautiful sea, jade green and deadly, would take me too. For a moment I considered plunging into it, making some last desperate bid for life or quick death. Better to die that way than tortured to death on a rock-face. I was frozen already, but it seemed a better bet than a hermit without a face ...

The waves were quicker now, rolling in, devouring. Cruel but impersonal sea. Soon I wouldn't be able to stand. It would hurl me to my knees, then against the rock-face, and when I was a pulpy broken mass, beyond fight or consciousness, its powerful suction would drag me into the pool to join the other dreadful occupant. And when I was quite dead, if there wasn't room for both of us, the ebb tide would carry me far away into the North Sea.

'Julie.' The hallucinations of drowning were starting early. I was sure someone had called my name. Perhaps this was the prelude to seeing all one's past life go past. There would be the happiness of early days in Corham, the bookshop with jackets crisp and new, smelling of adventure, and wonderful worlds to explore. There would be Mum and Dad smiling, and new scones baking, and autumn fires in the garden. And Charlie—and death.

And Adam—and death.

'Julie.' The voice was real. Above my head.

And little more than a whisper above the sea's roar. But quite real.

'Julie.' For a moment I thought it was Adam. Adam, oh my love ... Then I remembered he was dead. And I had killed him.

'Julie. Rope.' A tasselled grey cord of silk or nylon dangled above my head. The kind of cord a hermit might use on a cassock's waist.

'Hurry, Julie. Tide. No—time.' I took the end of the rope and whoever held the other end of it pulled. I yelled and let go, cried out:

'I can't. I hurt my wrist when I fell.'

The rope dangled down again. 'Tie ends—waist. But hurry, hurry.' I did as I was told, slowly, hampered by my injured wrist. 'Now—foothold. Try. Hold on.' But the rock-face was sheer green hell. Once, twice, thrice. Each time I fell back, sobbing against the taut rope.

'Ledge—see—to right.' I moved along, found a foothold.

'Good. Hang on. Got you ...'

I looked up into the hooded face of the Hermit. Then I lost my nerve. He had rescued me, but for what reason? I had killed Adam. Had he some other death in store for me, something terrible, more horrible than clean drowning?

'No, no!' I screamed. 'Let me go.'

'Julie. Please. Try—you can ...'

The desperation in his voice was sincere. If he was trying to save me, then he must be on my side. And fighting back fear I made one last effort. Fell back, bruised and aching. Tried again. There were words of encouragement, then I was lying face down, heaving myself up the last two feet out of the sea and on to the ledge. Untying the rope.

But where was the Hermit? Then I saw he was crawling away from me, dragging himself back along the ledge towards the distant entrance of the cave. Suddenly he stopped, moaned. His breathing was loud, louder than the sea below us. It wasn't only exertion. This was something much, much worse.

I scrambed towards him, all fear gone. He had tried to save my life for some obscure reason, although he and Adam had killed my father.

He heard me coming, turned. 'Stay away. Don't come near. Julie, for God's sake, don't come.' In a supreme effort he lifted one hand, dragged part of the hood over the lower part of his face. And as I looked down on his ravaged countenance, the pale flickering light hid most of the horror and some strange fleeting resemblance to the man he had once been, returned. 'Back there, Julie. Away from me. Talk.

Not much time. Finished. I was finished long ago. Dead man, Julie. Don't come nearer, just listen. Don't you understand, child. I'm a leper ...'

And as we waited, trapped but safe, above the tide, sometimes he talked, sometimes the words were washed away by the incoming tide, but I pieced together most of what he wanted to tell me.

And all the time I listened helplessly, because there was nothing else I could do. Soon there was nothing anyone could do and he was dead long before the rescuers, led by Philip Riche and Strachan, arrived down the tunnel. To carry him home ...

Among the police and fire brigade who arrived on the scene of the inferno which blazed through Whitton Peel late that night was Warren Browne. The whole place went up like a glorious tinder-box. They came too late ... As it was intended they should.

In Priory House Philip Riche bandaged my wrist and said to Marie, who had just arrived back from Berwick by taxi, 'She had best go home to Corham. She's still in shock, you know. Best tell your policeman friend you fell off Starlight,' he added to me.

I protested that I wanted to stay with Marie. Pale but composed, she said: 'I'll be all right, really.' She lifted a hand from the wheel of her chair and Philip grasped it firmly. 'You see, I have Philip now. Thank God we can start some kind of life together, a hundred miles from Whitton Sands.' She shivered. 'Philip isn't needed here any longer, now that *he's* dead.'

So I went back with Warren and by next morning the newspapers had the story. 'Hermit perishes in Mystery Inferno. A charred body, believed to be that of Jim Elliott, was recovered from the debris after the blaze which totally destroyed ancient Whitton Peel last night ... Elliott, who was in his late fifties, had been a recluse since the end of World War II, where he saw service in the Tank Corps during the desert campaign ... he was wounded and severely burned ... Elliott was last seen alive in the garden of Whitton Peel yesterday afternoon, by the vicar, Rev. Mervyn Scales ...'

I was waiting for another headline. Two days later it appeared.

'Woman's Body on Beach. Whitton Sands was the scene of a double tragedy when yesterday the body of Mrs. Melanie Hebburn was washed ashore ... Mrs. Hebburn had been missing since the plane, belonging to wealthy farmer, Mr. Bob Myers, in which she was passenger crashed into the sea off Holy Island ... Mr. Myer's body and part of the wreckage were recovered soon after the accident ... Mrs. Hebburn's body was identified by her husband, artist Mr. Adam Hebburn, of Priory House ... his head still bandaged after injuries received two days ago in a gallant but vain attempt to save hermit Jim Elliott from the fire which destroyed Whitton Peel ...'

Warren put down the paper. 'How ghastly,' he said. 'Poor Julie, this must be awful for you. It's always worse when it's people you know.'

'People you knew.' Warren was right in his past tense too. I'd probably never see any of them again. Only my dreams still yearned ...

It was all finished. All past. Warren had been wonderful. Perhaps with Adam Hebburn's brief episode in my life ended I could learn to love him. I hoped so. Twice he had tried hard to help my anxious parents gather up the threads of my life again. Now as we watched television together and saw men walking on the moon their adventures seemed a little tame after all that had befallen me at Priory House.

I thought of the other story that could never be told. How when Jim Elliott died of pneumonia, Hector had assumed his identity. And how Whitton Sands had kept faith with Hector Pleys and his secret, right to the end.

'The kind of end the heroes of old planned for themselves, Julie. They have my instructions, to the letter. It will be my most dramatic role,' he had whispered in the cave that night, as he lay dying. 'My greatest role. What a pity to play it to such a limited audience ...'

The doctor and the vicar played their parts and while the loyal servant Strachan struck a fire in Whitton Peel, they carried him into the great stone hall and laid him on his funeral pyre on the ancient wooden table, covered by the purple velvet robe he had once worn as King Arthur.

The tunnel leading back to Priory House was obliterated by falling masonry (helped by explosives), but first Melanie's body was recovered from the rock-pool by Strachan and Philip and concealed in a fishing boat until the fire was over. There must be no thread connecting the two incidents. Then together they 'discovered' her body on the beach ...

Time passed and one day when I was alone in the house the doorbell rang. Through the glass there was something white and shiny beyond the garden gate. A car. A white Kharmann Ghia and I opened the door to Adam

298

Hebburn.

I was shaking. After having prepared so many speeches should we ever meet again, I found I had nothing left to say. We stared at each other, speechless.

'I'm on my way to the crypt at Pleys Castle,' he said stiffly, 'to bury Hector's ashes. He would have wanted you to be there. Are you fit enough to face it now?'

So I went with him that cold dark afternoon to the family vault. Only Lady Ester was present and we shivered in a biting winter wind as Rev. Scales laid Hector's ashes to rest. And all around us as he prayed the dead leaves scuffled, like the secret ghostly footfalls of a forgotten army marching.

We walked back to the car and Adam drove to The Cloisters in silence.

'Won't you come in for a cup of tea or something?' I asked politely, hoping he would refuse. What was there left to say to this strange man at my side? Stranger, more remote today than the Horseman of Ninespears Crag, or my beloved Crusader, dead in his tomb for eight hundred years, had ever been.

He hesitated and I thought he was going to refuse. Then: 'All right, but just for a minute,' he said, and followed me into the lounge.

As I closed the door, he turned to face me, unsmiling. 'Well, Julie?'

'Well, Adam ...'

For a moment we looked at each other. Then like two blind people we groped for each other's arms.

Much later he said: 'So where do we go from here? Darling, I've tried like hell to keep out of your way, God knows I loathed the whole awful business of deceiving you. Especially when I knew you loved and trusted me. I urged him to tell you the truth, but he would have none of it. He wanted you to be impressed by your father, the great Hector Pleys, and after he knew how the Hermit sickened and horrified you he couldn't bear you to know that he was dying of leprosy, the leprosy he took on that long-ago ill-fated location in Africa. His other "injuries" were pure invention. He knew what he was in for, and was so terrified any of us would get it, he even had the tunnel rigged, so that communications could be made without contamination.'

He touched the healing scar on his head. 'I deserved that. No, don't say you're sorry—I'm not. At least it's something to remember you by.'

'Remember me by?'

'Well, what else? How could I ask you to love me, to trust me now?'

'Try me, Adam. You try asking me.'

He kissed me and said: 'Remember what I told you about being tied. If you marry me, I'll never let you go ...'

And so I became a farmer's wife, after all. Grandpa Hebburn died soon after Marie and Philip were married. So Adam Hebburn, painter, is also Adam Hebburn, farmer, and in a busy life with reasonable success in both occupations he has found himself and happiness again.

Priory House is a hotel now and Whitton Sands, with inn and tearoom and ancient Priory, its walk along the cliffs and summer sailing trips through the caves and around the Farne Islands, has long been one of Northmberland's most popluar tourist attractions.

Adam and I rarely talk about Hector these days. But recently there was another revival of his films on television. Our children were convulsed, thought Hector a riot. But, sadly, not in quite the way he would have hoped. To them, the peregrine who looked like Hereward was the star of *Hadrian*, the real excitement ...

For a while after they had gone to bed and the house was silent, Adam and I relived a little of that past and how, as he lay dying, I had held his hand. 'Leper or no, I was all he had,' I said.

But I have never told even Adam all the leper told me that night, just before he died. Because I still want—and try—to forget.

Soon after the plane crash in which it was presumed she had died, Melanie walked into Whitton Peel. 'We had never been close as father and daughter should be,' Hector said. 'Perhaps we were too much alike. Too ruthless. Perhaps all the women I had loved and discarded got their revenge when I had a daughter like her. Anyway, she was bored with Whitton Sands, and Adam. Willing to disappear for good if I would make it worth her while. Otherwise the Sunday papers might be very interested in the life and fake death of Hector leys ...

'I decided to help her. Told her I had money hidden from Adam, in the caves. It was hers. We walked along this ledge we're on now, Julia. Down there, I told her, in the rock-pool. She leaned over. "Where, I can't see anything?" "But you will, Melanie, you will." She turned, saw my face, screamed and staggered back. Into the pool.

'She never moved after she fell. Possibly her

neck was broken by the fall. I never touched her. I swear it on my dying breath ... But even if I could have saved her by stretching out my hand, I would have let her drown ... Drown or burn. There's no other way with witches ...

'And Adam had named her well. I watched her with him over the years. Watched her destroy first of all the boy I loved like my own son, then the artist I had discovered and given to the world ...

'The real Adam Hebburn was dead. And she had killed him.'